Special thanks to my wife Elaine for putting up with the long hours of writing madness and to Michael for giving me the key to unlock the door. What have you done!

The Abbot

David Moore

authorHOUSE®

AuthorHouse™
1663 Liberty Drive
Bloomington, IN 47403
www.authorhouse.com
Phone: 1-800-839-8640

This book is a work of fiction and, except in the case of historical fact, any resemblance to actual persons, living or dead, is purely coincidental.

This book is fully the work of David Moore and is protected under copyright as such.

First published by AuthorHouse   08/22/2011

ISBN: 978-1-4567-9373-9 (sc)
ISBN: 978-1-4567-9374-6 (ebk)

Printed in the United States of America

Any people depicted in stock imagery provided by Thinkstock are models, and such images are being used for illustrative purposes only. Certain stock imagery © Thinkstock.

This book is printed on acid-free paper.

Because of the dynamic nature of the Internet, any web addresses or links contained in this book may have changed since publication and may no longer be valid. The views expressed in this work are solely those of the author and do not necessarily reflect the views of the publisher, and the publisher hereby disclaims any responsibility for them.

CHAPTER 1

Marc squirmed and tried to move his legs as he lay in the wet grass. He had been concealed inside a gorse bush for the best part of two days now on an OP. Three feet away, to his left, lay his partner, Jay. Marc was observing the old, whitewashed Irish farmhouse and out buildings just west of Letterbrock, county Mayo, in the Irish Republic. He set down the Bressers binoculars and tried looking through the NUM Viper night scope but it was not yet dark enough.

'Any movement?',asked Jay.

'Nothing. Quiet as the grave'.

'Aye and cold as one too, you got the flask?.

Marc opened the Bergen rucksack and pulled out a thermos. Screwing off the lid he poured two cups and both men drank. The OP was far enough away that the hot steam coming from the cups would not betray their positions. Inside the Bergen were torches and a plethora of equipment, spare batteries, a satellite phone, digital camera and zoom lens, spare magazines for the Heckler and Koch G3 rifle that Jay was now holding. Jay was looking through the telescopic sight at the farmhouse, trying to establish if there was anyone at home when the faint noise of a car engine made both men freeze.

They tipped out the remainder of the hot coffee from their cups and settled in to see if the vehicle would stop at the farmhouse. Although they were far enough away

1

from it, the road ran close by and any vehicle would pass within a few yards of their OP. A minute later a Toyota Hi Ace van clattered along the road, slowing down, it turned into the farm lane and lurched and rocked it's way to the house. It stopped with a brake squealing in protest as a sticking brake calliper eventually won, forcing the van to a halt. One rear brake light burned brightly for a moment, the other staying unlit. Then all lights went out and the drivers' door opened. Marc had lifted the digital camera and was silently taking pictures. Jay stayed on target with his G3, just in case.

At the farm yard a lone male climbed out of the Toyota and made his way to the front door. He was an older man and had been tall in his younger days but was now starting to stoop forward. Fumbling in his pocket for a key, then the door opened after a short protest and he entered the house. The wooden front door had swollen with a mixture of age and Irish weather. He had to put his shoulder to it to gain entry. Once inside he switched on the kitchen light and pulled the old, dusty, moth eaten curtains. Wandering to the sink he turned the tap on and let the water run. Reaching for the kettle he watched it fill through the spout, then setting it on the gas stove lit the front ring. They would be here soon and he would welcome them with a freshly brewed cup. Irish hospitality he thought, after all they had travelled far.

To the left hand side of the stove were two copper water pipes. They exited the stove sidewall and turned through ninety degrees, running skyward, after six inches they entered a homemade wooden box. The box ran parallel to the kitchen wall and the pipes, hidden inside, eventually made their way to the roofspace as an express channel for the hot water. The wooden box they occupied had a small chrome knob on the underside, hidden from view. The man felt for the catch and in a well practised movement pushed it and a panel swung open. He pulled out a blanket which for many years had lived jammed between the two pipes. The pipes had been altered to accommodate the item many years ago. He set the blanket on the table and rolled it out. An American Springfield M1 carbine rifle lay inside the blanket. He gently lifted it and removed the fifteen shot, empty, magazine.

Reaching into his trouser pocket he pulled out a small canvas bag. Tipping its contents out onto the table top he counted ten long brass rounds of .30 calibre. He loaded the magazine carefully and then slipped it on to the M1. Cocking the weapon. He made sure the safety catch was on. This model was very old and had only the single shot capability. Later M1's came with a fully automatic function, an absurd idea, he thought. If you want a machine gun then buy a machine gun.

He surveyed the old table top and remembered all the variety of weapons that the Provisional IRA had stripped there. All the discussions about assembly and range, rate of fire and stopping power. The first weapons had been M1 carbines and M1 Garands from the last war. Sent by well wishers from America. Later M16 Colts or the Armalite as the news reels called them. The widowmaker. They came in several variations, CAR 15's, Colt Commandos, AR 15's. Some Ruger Mini 14's had arrived too, the Remington Woodmaster and an assortment of .30-06 and .223 ammunition. Then the suppliers changed to the Middle East. Libya. AK47's in all their various guises arrived. Their short, fat 7.62 rounds and banana shaped magazines. M60 heavy machine guns, two Barrett light 50 cal rifles and a soviet made Dushka .50 cal heavy machine gun. All had been over this very table top at one time or another. Aye, he thought, pistols and machine pistols too, of all makes and models.

He remembered the training weekends for the volunteers. He would run them through dry drills with empty weapons. Make ready. Make safe. He would shout and roar. Watch and shoot. Stoppage, he would yell, then watch as the class would cock, lock and look. Cock the weapon, lock the working parts to the rear and look into the chamber and magazine housing. He would give the stoppage type. No rounds in the magazine, no rounds in the chamber, he'd say. Empty mag they would all chime back in a well rehearsed prayer like voice. Reload, he would bellow, watching the fumbling as they tried to remove the old mag only to replace it with a pretend fresh magazine, full of imaginary rounds. Reloading was always good, as the more nervous fumble with the mag, dropping it, letting it clatter to the floor. Or not to fully push home the fresh mag only to find it falling out in the later, make ready, drill. ''Dead men', he'd shout pointing at the fumblers. 'Dead as fucking Nelson', sort it out, he'd yell. Aye, those were good days. He had enjoyed them. Proper weapons with different quirks; the Ruger Mini 14 needed the mag tilted away from the weapon to extract it properly. The M16 with its dust flap, located over the ejector port, snapping open as the weapon was cocked. Some students would try to fool him, pretending that they were ready to fire but the closed dust flap always betrayed them.

The sound of an approaching car engine made him lift the M1 carbine and move to the door.

Outside the farm house Marc and Jay watched as the BMW five series drove along the lane and into the yard. A tall man, in his mid fifties got out and stretched. Pushing both arms out at right angles to his body then lifting them to head height, pushing his chest forward and straightening up. He appeared to be filling his lungs with fresh air after a long journey. Eventually he exhaled and his breath could be clearly seen from their OP. It hung in the frosty night air like some cartoon thought bubble. He was wearing a long black coat and appeared to have a suit on underneath it. Strolling to the car boot and opened it, reaching in and pulling out an aluminium case. Slamming the boot closed he walked to the door which was pulled open and the older, taller man appeared, carrying the M1 carbine for all to see. Marc heard Jay inhale then exhale slowly and he knew he was now on target. Jay was aiming right at the gunman.

In the distance, at the farm house, both men shook hands. Then they proceeded inside closing the door and shutting off the yellow glow made by the kitchen light. The light had spilled out from the house illuminating the dark and welcoming the new guest, it was as if the house was pleased to see old comrades again. The yard returned to the gun metal grey of approaching night. All gone back to normal, or was it? The faint drone of a motorcycle engine could just be heard above the wind kissed gorse hissing to and fro. It was getting louder and louder all the time.

CHAPTER 2

A gaggle of drunks stood outside the front doors of the Silver Tavern, in High Street, Antrim. They were all smoking cigarettes, huddled together in little groups, coat collars turned up to keep out the bitter chill. They drew upon the cigarette butts with all the fervour of the condemned man having his last puff. All eager to return to the warm, welcoming public house yet still having to spend a few precious minutes trying to satisfy their cravings.

A thick set man with a shaved head pushed past them and entered the pub. At the crowded bar he squeezed his way to the front and held up his ten pound note hoping it would be noticed. It was.

'What'll it be', asked the ruddy faced bar tender.

'Guinness and a vodka and white'.

'Pint?'

'Aye, sorry a pint. And have one yourself'.

'Cheers, I'll get a pint at the end of the night'.

The drinks were set up and the bar man smiled, revealing his yellow stained teeth. The baldy man leaned closer to him and asked;

'Mickey Doyle about?'

'Who's asking?'.

'Tell him it's The Abbot'.

'Did you say Abbot',

'Aye that's it'.

The barman turned away disappearing through the connecting door and into the back room. Sean Donovan had been known as The Abbot for more years than he cared to remember. It seemed that he looked like an Abbot because of his shaven head and rotund shape. Big Eddie had been first to christen him and it was to become his finest name. Big Eddie was not the sharpest tool in the shed and seldom spoke any words of wisdom, but everyone agreed that this was his finest name. So it was The Abbot became The Abbot for ever. The barman returned and lifted the counter top at the corner of the bar motioning for The Abbot to follow him. In the dimly lit back room sat a small, stout man. He was in the company of two attractive young ladies, all were seated on a red leather sofa which had seen better days. It was a high button back type with roll top arms all held in place by neat rows of small brass studs, many of which were now missing. The man stood up and stretched out his chubby hand. Both men shook hands.

'Mr Donovan, you come highly recommended'.

'Thanks', the Abbot replied.

'Have a seat', with that the two ladies got up and returned to the bar through the connecting corridor.

'Mr Doyle, what's all this about?'.

'Please, call me Mickey. Everyone does.'.

'OK, Mickey. I'm a wee bit bewildered as to why you wanted to see me. I thought Morgan had paid the money?'.

'He did. Oh it's nothing to do with him. I have a problem I hope you can help me with'.

'What's that?'

'I was expecting a package to be delivered yesterday. It's an aluminium case. I was told that it would be arriving at Dublin docks. It has disappeared and I need a finder to bring it to me. Are you up for that?'

'What's in it, or shouldn't I ask?'

'You shouldn't ask'.

'Ok, fair enough'.

'It's only fair to tell you that it's of interest to other parties'.

'What sort?'.

'The sort with guns. Both legal ones and illegal ones'.

'OK. Did you get told a price?'.

'Aye, there's no problem on that score. You taking any one with you?'.

'No Mickey. I work better on my own.'

'Right O. Here's a mobile number for me and the second number is the guy who last had the case. The address is where the handover should have taken place. See what you can find out'. Mickey handed a business card to the Abbot, the numbers and address were written on the plain side in black biro. Then Mickey leaned forward and asked;

'Are you as good as they say you are?'.

'Depends who's saying it'.

'Did you really take out Geordie Cross and those boys on you're own?'

'Well, lets say they were in the way and business is business'.

'Fucking hell. Geordie was a psycho'.

'Was he. I only met him once and as I say he was in the way. Anyway, I'd better go and see if I can solve you're problem?'.

The Abbot stood up and made his way back through to the bar. The barman pointed to the two drinks he had left earlier. A few minutes later the Abbot was on his way.

He remembered Geordie and his boys. That was the price you paid for attention to detail or lack of it in Geordies case. The Abbot had been contracted to kill a guy called Halliday who had taken shelter with Geordie and his three heavies. All were UVF or had been at one time or another. The Abbot tracked them to a house in Rathcoole, a few miles from Belfast and had shot them all in the kitchen as they ate their fish and chip suppers. He had followed one home from the Golden Glen Chip Emporium on the O'Neil Road and watched him enter the house. The Abbot went to the kitchen window and saw all five crowded into the tiny room around an old yellow formica topped table. The Abbot had two pistols, both Browning Hi-Powers, nine millimetre with fourteen round magazines.

Kicking open the kitchen door he remembered the look of astonishment on their fat chip feeding faces. The smell of chips and vinegar mixed with the cordite and gunpowder discharge, the noise of furniture crashing to the floor, gunshots, shouts and screams all muddled together. The milk carton clipped by the bullets, spilling it's contents onto the cheap laminate flooring where it mixed with the blood of the victims. Red and white. Then the stark silence. Halliday lay on the floor with the others, Job done, he thought. He had noticed two of the men were carrying pistols. So devastating and sudden was the attack that they never had a chance to draw them. One was an old Webley .38 revolver, the other a modern CZ nine millimetre. The Abbot pulled them out of the trouser waistbands of both victims and took them with him when he left. The entire incident had taken less than a minute yet so many lives had been lost. He had always been gifted at killing. Seven years in the British army had not been wasted. Walking calmly away from the scene he made his way to the shore at Jordanstown where he tossed the two pistols into Belfast lough. From that night on he had become the stuff of legend. Regarded as a man who gets the job done. A man of his word, a man not to be taken lightly and he liked that idea. Stories abounded that he ate the fish and chips left by the victims. Others said he made tea among the bodies in the small kitchen. In truth the kitchen was so crowded that the men were standing up eating. All this had worked in his favour as none of them had time to react or see a clear target. The Abbot did nothing to dispel the stories and now everyone gave him a wide berth and plenty of street respect.

When the ceasefire broke out in Ulster the dynamic changed drastically. Sure, the leading republican and loyalist leaders got on the peace train. Into the first class carriage. Now wearing expensive suits and with trips to the USA and further. Fresh new haircuts and grooming, like prize poodles at a show. Unfortunately the rest of the paramilitaries couldn't all get into the first class carriage. Some were pushed into the attached cattle trucks and some even missed the train altogether. They still carried on like small mafia gods in their own areas, teaming up on occasion with their opposite numbers in the opposing faction to carry out a job. Then the Chinese came. Triads, growing cannabis all over Ireland. They supplied and distributed everywhere. The old paramilitaries got their share. Their slice of the cake. At first it was a large slice and it looked like they all may get along. Then the first Russian mafia arrived. They brought girls from the former Soviet Union, opened brothels, not in the deprived run down areas of Belfast but the more select. They were making eight or nine thousand pounds per week and were not afraid of a few old Provos or Loyalist thugs. Sure they still got their slice of the cake from the Russians, but now it was only a mouthful. The Russians were careful not to upset too many people, but inevitably they did and so job vacancies for men like the Abbot sprang up. He killed without question for money. He collected, delivered and never asked too much. Both sides in Northern Ireland feared him, the Russians liked that. They paid him well for his work, he enjoyed it, it was a win, win situation as the Americans say.

It wasn't only Loyalists that the Abbot hit, oh no. Just after the Geordie Cross incident he was contracted by the Provo High Command for a wee bit of housekeeping. A guy called Malachy McCartan, or Big Mal as the locals knew him had crossed the PIRA commanders and had to be taught a lesson. He had two sons and had lived in the Andersonstown area of Belfast all his life. The oldest son, Michael, had moved to Galway and married his child hood sweetheart. He ran a number of vans, delivering all over Ireland, mostly in the Republic. He was uninterested in the IRA or the struggle, too busy trying to make a crust. The second son, Finbar, was unmarried and lived at home with his parents. He was, as they say in Belfast, a bit soft in the head. A wee bit slow on the uptake and not very bright at school, unable to keep a job. It appears that Finbar was accused of indecent behaviour with two school girls, it had happened in the local park. The police were not called but the Provos did pay him a visit. Two men had beaten him in an alleyway just off the Falls Road. In his attempt at escape he had dashed across the road and been hit by a Volvo car. Finbar was in a coma in the Royal Victoria hospital for months.

His father, Big mal, was outraged and although he was a Provo himself he found one of his son's assailants and almost beat him to death. Despite the fact that Finbar's beating had been ordered, Big Mal was not having it. So a precedent had been set and broken. The IRA were on ceasefire and therefore unable to do any housekeeping of this magnitude. Enter the Abbot. He accepted the job and one Wednesday afternoon he drove a Peugeot Speedflight scooter to Milltown cemetery. Here he waited on Big Mal, who was laying flowers at his mother's grave. The Abbot shot Mal in the face and head several times in broad daylight, then calmly climbed aboard the scooter and buzzed away. Job done.

The Abbot was the product of a mixed marriage. His proper name was Sean Alexander Donovan. His father was a protestant and his mother a Roman Catholic, although neither cared too much for church and seldom attended. His uncle was a lay preacher in the local Baptist church and had disowned his brother when he married outside his religion. Sean went to a Roman catholic primary school and in the later years he was tormented and bullied by the older catholic boys in the school and the district, after they discover his father was a protestant. The present round of the troubles had escalated to fever pitch and his father, after losing his job, was forced to flee to a harder, tougher, Protestant area.

Here, young Sean was forced to change his name to Alexander Donovan and sent to the local secondary school. Several weeks after he started the boys found the role call and saw him listed as Sean Alexander. More bullying and beatings ensued. He became more and more withdrawn, quiet, shy and very, very angry. This lasted until the summer where he turned fifteen. He had been spending a lot of time at a local gym, body building mostly and weight lifting. Although he was under age the gym owner liked him and knew the torment he faced, so he gave him a summer job and allowed him to train.

Returning to school, Sean was now a lot stronger and more confident that the previous year. One Tuesday morning three of his main tormentors found him in the playground and started to push him and punch him as they did every other time. Something inside Sean's head snapped. An awakening. A switch thrown on that could never again be turned off. Grabbing the biggest tormentor he pushed his thumb into his eye socket, holding him by the back of his head as he did so. Despite the other two boys beating and beating him, he held on. He felt the eyeball pop, yet he still pushed and pushed. Everyone recoiled in horror when he released the lad. While the other two bullies were helping their friend, Sean had run into the school building and pulled a small two litre fire extinguisher off the corridor wall, returning with it to the playground. He smacked one of the bullies across the face, breaking his nose with the extinguisher. The other bully tried to run but to no avail. He too was beaten, savagely and badly. When the teachers finally arrived and restrained Sean, he was smiling. He enjoyed it. He really, really enjoyed it. He was suspended. After six weeks he was allowed back to school. Another similar incident forced his expulsion, this time for good. Police were involved and the Juvenile scheme set up. The bullies refused to press charges, even the one with the badly injured eye. His eye never fully recovered. Sean received little more that a caution for the attacks.

Sean left home on his sixteenth birthday and joined the army. He was a boy soldier and had signed up for nine years in the Royal Engineers. He enjoyed the training and fought his corner with the best of them whenever he needed to. He completed 'P Company 'training, tough paratrooper training at Aldershot. Sean would be parachuted into the front line as an engineer, skilled at demolition and combat together. Although he was still in the Royal Engineers he could wear the parachute wings so envied by the other units of the army. Sean saw active service in several theatres and it was during a rescue mission in Africa that he killed his first man. He liked it too. Same buzz as the playground. More killings followed. He disliked peacetime and so upon leaving the army early, placed an advert in Soldier of Fortune magazine. Soon he was back as a civilian security guard only with an AK47 in the middle east. More missions followed, each slightly more dangerous than the last. His employers became frightened by his attitude, or rather lack of it. He never showed any remorse or thought for victims or assailants that crossed his path. When the opportunity presented itself they released him from his contract.

So back to Belfast for the Abbot. However, a man such as this remains unemployed for a very short while. So it came to pass that there were always job vacancies that only he could fill. This briefcase recovery was just another one.

CHAPTER 3

Marc and Jay huddled down inside the gorse bush and scanned the black horizon for any sign of the approaching vehicle. At last they caught sight of yellow lights in a field just off to the right of the farmhouse. It was a square shaped, yellow coloured light. It was travelling across the field toward the road and the old wrought iron gate. A second light came into view a short distance behind the first. Looking through the night scope Marc saw that there were two farm bikes. Quads, travelling quite slowly and deliberately. Both quads had two people on board. Must be big four strokes, he thought. Maybe four hundred cc or bigger. The bikes slipped down into the natural dip between the field and the road, hidden from view behind the dry stone wall.

Jay was on target now with the G3. He had a round in the chamber of the 7.62 semi automatic rifle but his fire select lever remained at safe. No chances taken. Jay had spent five years in the SAS as an operative and was a counter terrorist specialist. This was his natural habitat. Inside a gorse bush. On a dark, cold and desolate night. Jay had been seconded to the US Navy Seals for two years. He had seen action with them in Iraq and in Africa too. He fitted in well, standing at six foot four and being well built to boot. He loved training in the gym, the pool, road runs and shooting. That was his passion. Now as he scanned the dry stone wall, looking through his night sight the first potential target appeared.

Four men, all dressed in black and wearing ski masks dropped silently onto the tarmac road. One after the other. Shadows, darting across the road and into the farmyard. Each was carrying a sub machine pistol of some sort. Straining through the sight, Jay, was almost certain they had MP5's but at this distance several makes and models look the same. He deduced that they were nine millimetre machine pistols and that would have to do for now. At the corner of the house one man stopped and knelt down. He was covering the direction that they had just come from and the gateway to the road.

Another man made a wide circle away from the group, passing close by the BMW car. He knelt at the front of the vehicle, covering the fields and outhouses to the left of the farmhouse. The remaining two went to each side of the farmhouse door, standing with their backs to the wall. Then the man on the left swung into the door. It burst inward and both men rushed inside, a shaft of yellow glow shone from the door, flooding part of the yard. The house appeared to have been startled. Seconds later there were three bursts of automatic gunfire from inside. Jay and Marc could see the white flashes through the old curtains. Split second flashes. Like a lightning strike in the distance. Sheet lightning. Flash flash. Then the dim glow returned to the curtain covered window.

The two men rushed out, one carrying the aluminium case that had arrived in the BMW earlier. All four were gone in seconds. Back across the road, over the stone wall. The sound of two quads starting and then they pulled off into the distance. Jay could have shot them easily. He would have taken at least two. Possibly three, he thought, but two most definitely.

Marc pulled himself up and turned to Jay.

'Cover me. I need a closer look'. Jay nodded.

Slipping out of the bush he drew his nine millimetre Glock pistol and with a firm grip on the butt, began to scurry toward the house. Mr Wilner had been most exact in the briefing. Observe, film, photograph but do not get involved. Marc needed to know if the men were dead. Jay had broken cover too. He moved on a parallel course to Marc, stopping a few yards short of the house. The G3 tight into his shoulder. The fire selector now on single shot. Finger on the trigger. Ready, ready.

Marc sprinted across the concrete yard and stopped short of the door. Leaning against the wall, he looked into the open doorway. He could see a black boot, attached to a leg. Walking on the balls of his feet he crept further in. The elder of the two men lay face down in an ever widening pool of dark blood. Most of his wounds seemed to be in his back. It looked like he had been shot extensively with the first burst. An upturned chair lay on the far side of a rickety old table. A right leg stuck out at a strange angle, half hidden by the table. Walking in closer Marc now looked over the table top. The well dressed BMW driver lay on his back, arms outstretched. He had been sitting at the table and the gunfire had made him fall backwards, taking the chair with him. He too was dead. His chest and face having taken most of the gunshots. An old M1 Carbine lay on the tabletop along with two cups of hot tea. Marc pulled two DNA swab kits from his trouser pocket. Breaking open the sterile tubes he drew out the cotton bud inside. He first swabbed BMW man. Poking the bud inside his mouth. Then he replaced the bud in the container, screwing the lid on tightly. The same operation was carried out on the second victim. All the while Jay stayed outside. Covering. Watching. Waiting. The faint glow of car headlights on the roadway got his attention.

'Marc', he shouted.

Marc appeared at the door, seeing the lights too. Both men dashed into the field and began to scramble back toward the OP.

A silver Ford Mondeo drew up in the yard and three men climbed out. Marc was close to the OP but unable to get back to his previous position inside the bush. He collected his things, the camera and the Viper nightscope. Placing them silently into his Bergen. He could not see Jay but he knew that he would be covering him. As soon as he was packed he quietly crawled to the gap in the dry stone wall. Silently pushing the Bergen through and slipping through behind it. Now on the road he felt exposed. He sat up, pulling on the heavy rucksack, holding his pistol and stooping forward he began a silent jog away from the farm house. He heard voices in the distance. Glancing back he could see torch light beams scanning across the sky and the stone wall. He ran faster. The gateway appeared on his left several minutes later. Darting through it he paused. Controlling his breathing. Calm, calm. In and Out. In and out. Now looking back he could no longer see the torch beams. Movement caught his eye. He saw him on the far side of the stone wall. The bobbing of his head. Then up and over. Jay landed silently and with all the grace of a gazelle opposite the gate way. He grinned.

'Time to go I think'. He whispered.

Marc nodded. They followed the path from the gate for several hundred yards. In the overgrown lane leading to an old derelict farm building they saw the Nissan X-Trail parked and waiting. Jay opened the drivers door, the interior bulb had been removed so the vehicle was not illuminated inside. Quickly stashing the kit in the rear seat they pulled off their wet camouflage clothing and got inside. Jay started the two litre diesel and they pulled quietly away, out of the lane and headed for home. Ballyclare, in Northern Ireland and their safe house in the Dale.

'Any ideas who the two in the house were Marc?'

'No. None. I've got their DNA so we can check'.

'What about those guys on the quads?'

'Again Jay no. No aint got a clue. They were slick though. Good, very professional'.

'You said it'.

Three hours later the Nissan pulled into RAF Aldergrove and Jay presented his ID to the bored squaddie on the front gate. Marc had made the phone call to the firm and a Bell helicopter stood waiting on the apron beside the SAS hangar behind the church. The chopper was silent and the four rotor blades hung down in a crescent shape like giant long ears. Their tips faintly moving in the early morning breeze. At the office, just inside the hangar a male made his way out to meet the Nissan.

'Mr Jay', he said,'long time no see'.

'Mr Adam'. Grinned Jay,'How goes it?'

The DNA samples were handed over along with the film disc and digital camera.

'You have a new housemate', grinned the pilot.

A tall thin blond woman in her late twenties was standing in the doorway of the office. She held up her hand in a high five style.

'Hi, I'm Miss Jenny', she beamed. Marc and Jay looked at each other for a split second, both thinking the same thing; another bloody woman for the safe house. Just what we need.

CHAPTER 4

The old Saab 95 rolled along Belfast's Shankill Road, turning into Joymount Street and stopping close to number fifty eight. The Abbot bounced the car up onto the kerb, reversing back awkwardly, leaving the wheels turned to the right on full lock. He locked the car, pausing as he walked away, he looked at the tyre tread on the drivers front wheel. Time to buy tyres he thought. A few seconds later he was hammering on the door of number fifty eight.

The door of the two up, two down, mid terrace house opened to reveal a tall, slim man in his mid forties. He smiled, his lips curling back underneath a bushy, black moustache revealing his yellow teeth. His dark hair was slicked back, like something from a Brylcream advert. That Elvis Presley look.

'Abbot', he exclaimed, 'Come on in'.

'All right brigadier', said Abbot.

Jim McClean had been known as the Brigadier since he left the regular army some twelve years ago. He worked on Apollo Road, unloading fruit and vegetable trucks four days a week. Early starts at around four thirty in the morning meant an eleven am finish and the rest of the day was his. At weekends he was a sergeant instructor in the Territorial Army at Kinnegar barracks, Holywood. He taught the recruits to fire rifles and the famous GPMG, heavy machine gun. Most weekends he went to Longton MOD base at Carlisle or Faslane navy camp in Scotland and trained on the ranges. The training programme had recently been stepped up with the Iraq situation and the ongoing war in Afghanistan. He loved his weekends and was proud of his recruits.

'What brings you up the Shankill then?'

'Wee social call. Well I need some stuff too if you have any?'

'For you Abbot there is always stuff. I take it you mean nines?'

'Aye,please'.

The Brigadier opened the door underneath the stairs and after a few minutes returned with a bag of nine millimetre pistol rounds. At the weekends on the range the army kept a tight record of all the 7.62 and 5.56 ammunition that they used. The wars were using up rounds at a phenomenal rate and so accurate issue and return were vital on the training ranges. Each recruit had been issued with a reduced number of SA80 rounds, so precise training was essential. The Brigadier signed and countersigned all issues. Each fire drill on the range was overseen by MOD personnel and, on Occasion, Military Police. The MP's searched the odd kit bag for spare rounds after the firing was over as it was an offence under military law to hold live ammunition in camp. Any recruit caught would be tried by a military court and be sent to the military prison at Aldershot. They raided the lockers sometimes too, there was no excuse accepted. Firers on the range sign a declaration at the end of the practice stating that they do not hold any live ammunition nor do they know of any not accounted for.

Not so for the pistol ammunition, however. The old nine millimetre rounds were kept in a small metal dustbin and loaded when required. Not every one was trained in the Browning pistol only those who were officers, cooks or clerks were allowed to carry it. The officers were trained in the pistol on a separate course. So as long as a few magazines were fired off everyone was happy. The Brigadier allowed four magazines to each student, but in reality they only fired two or three magazines on the Sunday morning shoot. The recruits played five a side football before lunch on Sundays and that cut short the pistol training. So every now and then the Brigadier could bring a handful of rounds home. He did this by slipping a full magazine into his kitbag, if caught he could lie and say it must have fallen in by accident. Once home he would unload the magazine and return it empty on his next weekend away. Easy. Over the years he had built up a considerable amount of ammunition which he had hidden all over Belfast in various locations. Ten rounds here, twenty rounds there and there were always customers too. Men like the Abbot who were willing to pay over the odds for such stuff.

'There you go Abbot'. He said returning and tossing a bag onto the sofa.

'How many?'.

'About forty. There are some hollow point in that too'.

'Cheers'.

'Want a cuppa?'

'Aye. I'll take a tea'.

The Brigadier arose and walked to the kitchen, switching on the kettle. He shouted back;

'How do you take it, NATO standard?'

'Aye NATO will do. Milk and two please'.

23

The Abbot handed him a roll of crisp ten pound notes when he returned with the cups. Both men talked about past comrades and who they had recently been speaking with, who had died and who was still serving and where they were abroad or in England and a general catch up conversation unfolded. Then the Abbot asked him;

'Ever heard of Mickey Doyle?'

'Aye. Mickey Doyle. Aye. That the guy who was in the RA?'

'He would have been at a time. Think he's involved with someone else now?'

'Word on the street is he still into the bomb making. Wee Barry told me that Mickey had been in Syria or some of them desert places last year. I know he stopped the drugs after the Chinese escapade. Why, you working for him?'

'Sort of. He's asked me to do a wee job. Moneys in the bank like at the minute'.

'Be careful Abbot he's a hard bastard. Watch your back'.

'No worries Brigadier. Always do'.

'I'll ask about and see what I can turn up.'

'Thanks big lad, you're a gem'.

'Aye a diamond geezer as they say in Aldershot'.

Both men laughed. The Abbot drained his cup and reached it to the Brigadier. Bidding farewell at the door the Abbot returned to the Saab. Right, he thought, time to get two new tyres on then a journey to Southern Ireland.

CHAPTER 5

Eleanor Clarke placed one leg on the left hand pedal of her Raleigh Ladies bicycle and pushing off with her right leg gently pulled it through the low bar and began to pedal. The concrete lane from her office to the front gate was bumpy and in poor repair. The gate was a good country mile away. She was wearing her brown brogue shoes and a long denim skirt. Dark blue heavy woollen tights and her green short jacket. The large brown leather handbag, with the shoulder strap, draped across her body like a Sam Browne belt. A small Tupperware box rested on the rear chrome carrier. The remains of her frugal lunch, cottage cheese on rye bread, still inside it.

Leaving the Military Research laboratory building at Porton Down she reached the front gate. An armed MOD guard raised the red and white barrier and bid her goodnight. Hardly night, she thought, at five fifteen. She selected third gear with the finger selector on her Sturmey Archer Three speed gears, located on the handlebars. The bicycle was quite an age but it provided adequate transport and kept her carbon footprint low. Cars were for those other girls, the sort who drank and went with boys. The sort who got pregnant at sixteen and appeared on daytime television shows. Not for Eleanor. Oh no. Her late father, an army Colonel, always insisted that she stay indoors until all homework and later course work were completed. From she had been a little girl, the study and research ethic had been implanted in her brain. Now she was a leading scientist with the military at the chemical weapons plant at Porton Down. She had received a first class honours degree in chemistry and mathematics from Cambridge and over the years had several articles published in the' New Scientist' and 'Science to-day'. Lectures given by her at Yale and Harvard in the United States and the Pollock Institute in Geneva assured an undisputed knowledge of her subject. Her extended work researching chemical weapon systems and binary bomb delivery systems had guaranteed her a place in Porton Down for a very long time to come.

On the open road now she headed for the village of Winterbourne Gunner only a few miles away. Living alone, she was almost sixty and had only ever had one boyfriend. That heady summer in nineteen seventy one, now just a memory. He left, so long ago, father had not approved and that was that. She missed him sometimes. Eleanor had only one brother who was fifty and was a missionary in Africa. He was married and had two boys, both in their early teens. She loved them all too. She missed them.

A short while later, Eleanor arrived at her home. A red brick, small, country cottage with a stone wall at the front, hiding a small, neat garden. A simple garden gate was in the centre of the wall. It was ajar. She paused, it was never ajar. The postman she thought, he's forgotten to secure it. Well, I will write another letter to the post office manager. Hopefully that will ensure that the gate is properly closed. Honestly, these people, she thought. Wheeling her bicycle along the narrow gravel path and around to the rear of her cottage. She pushed it into the wooden lean-to at the rear of the house. A thin silver chain hung down with a small brass padlock attached at the end. Eleanor looped the chain around the frame and clipped the padlock shut with the deft ease that comes with many years of practice. The Raleigh was now a prisoner in it's lonely lean-to, until eight o'clock tomorrow morning. She too would soon be a prisoner in her cottage, in many ways, few neighbours ever came to visit and the local children stayed well away in case they incur her wrath. Heaven forbid the ball in the garden or any noise should intrude into her precious space.

Placing the old long key into the rear mortise door lock, Eleanor gave it a good turn anti-clockwise and the lock slid effortlessly open. Home, at last. Entering the kitchen she felt a sudden chill, a feeling that something was not just as it should be. The pine cupboards all neat and tidy, the Aga stove with the stainless steel tea pot on it and a small saucepan sitting on the draining board. A neat row of brightly coloured tea towels hung down from the drying rack on the Aga. They looked like flags on a yacht, smartly arranged, proudly setting out their message. What was it? Did they say welcome home Eleanor, lady of the house, or did they herald a warning? The scrubbed oak kitchen table with it's silver salt and pepper cellars in the centre and a small blue sugar bowl, covered with a lace doilie with little beads around the edge. The two oak chairs, one slightly pulled out from the table. No, all appeared as she had left it that morning at eight a.m. exactly.

Eleanor set her handbag on the table and walked into the neatly arranged front room. Her Dell tower computer and monitor were sitting on the small computer table by the window. She often researched items on it instead of watching television, another glimpse of her past. No good comes from watching too much TV her father had said. So she followed no soaps, no sporting events and only watched the news items now and again. Something moved quickly to her left. She caught the movement in her peripheral vision, as she turned her head something grabbed her from behind. A rough calloused hand went across her mouth, another around her waist. A smooth, faintly familiar, voice spoke;

'Eleanor, do not be alarmed. We don't wish to hurt you.'

She was frog marched to the easy chair and roughly pushed down into it. Her mouth was released and the grip changed to her two hands. Both were pushed firmly down onto the chair arms. Her attacker was a black man. She noted his black hands. East Africa, West Africa, she thought? He stood behind her, reaching over her shoulder, holding her down. She could smell his sweat and his breath stale with a mild garlic. She gagged slightly and felt her pulse racing, realising that struggling was futile she tried to calm her breathing.

'How dare you come . . . '. She began, but stopped short when the second man walked fully into the room. He too was black. He looked at her and she felt terror rising within her. A flood of emotion and fear, his eyes were deep and dark, like black pools, devoid of feeling, like those of a cobra. Eleanor was terrified for a split second but her breathing was helping her to be calm. As he stood before her, slightly swaying, she felt mesmerized like the rat caught in a cobra's dance just before it strikes. She noticed he was holding a videotape. He looked directly into her eyes and spoke.

'Eleanor. Please do not scream. I have no wish to hurt you but my colleague, well, that's another matter. Do you understand?'

Eleanor nodded. Her breathing was now slightly calmer, although she felt sick and her head was still swimming with a million thoughts and questions. The man continued;

'I wish for you to watch this video. I think you may know the people on it'.

All the while the man had been holding the VCR remote. She now saw that it was a video cover he held in his hand and not the tape. They had already loaded the VCR and had the TV turned on too. So, she thought, they must have been here a while. He pushed play and the image on screen flickered into life. It was a man tied up and badly beaten around the face. A copy of The Times newspaper was visible in the corner of the tape and the date could be clearly seen, it was two days previous. He was pleading with his off screen captor then looking directly into the camera. As his head turned from profile to full face Eleanor gasped aloud. It was her brother, she was transfixed. His eyes were swollen and his lips cut and bleeding, bruises along his cheeks and brow. He began to speak;

'Eleanor, for Gods sake do what they ask. They have Kyle, Mark and Ellie. Please Eleanor, please for Gods sake . . . .' The scene then changed. Still indoors, two boys could be seen, both tied and sitting with their backs against a wall. As the camera panned out a boy soldier complete with AK47, camouflage clothing and a much too large baseball cap on top of a shaven head was standing guard. He had the disconnected look of the stolen child, drugged, in a world of his own. In truth he was no different from the others, smoking Gnat and drinking home made wine, that make up Africa's one million boy soldiers. A generation taken from their villages as children and trained, beaten, drugged and given the AK with one common goal. Kill, kill, kill. Eleanor recognised her nephews on the tape and could feel the fear rising within her.

The camera stayed indoors and the next scene showed Ellie. Again tied up and sitting on an old school room chair with a metal frame and wooden seat and back. She too had been beaten. Again as the camera panned out three black soldiers were standing drinking beer beside her chair. One was stroking her hair and grinning at the cameraman. Eleanor choked back a tear, poor Ellie, she thought, poor dear Ellie.

'Your brother is in Mogadishu. In my country. Somalia. He is on a faith mission. We will release him when you deliver an item to us. If you don't deliver, well, then that is a very different set of circumstances'.

'What do you want. I have some money . . . . ?'

'Ha, please, Eleanor. El-ea-nor. We want an item from your work. GB'.

'GB?' repeated Eleanor.

'Yes GB or shall I say c4-h10-fo2p'.

'Sarin gas', she exclaimed,' Are you mad, even if I could get it how would you transport it. What would you do with it, it's so very complex?'

'You worked on the Sarin project with the Americans. Remember. The binary bomb. Please Eleanor do not insult my intelligence. I know we are a backward country, but we have done our homework.'

'You can't be serious?' she said.

'I am. We want the two components separated, the Methyphosohonyl put in the top of the container and the Isopropyl alcohol in the bottom '.

'What container?' she asked.

He walked out to the hallway and returned with a black plastic container. It was the size of a thermos flask and had two caps. One at each end. He tossed it onto her knee. At this point the second man released her. Composing herself she picked it up and examined it.

'It will melt this plastic in a matter of seconds', she began.

'Open it'.

She screwed off the plastic cap on one end. A metal flask had been fitted inside the container, it had a small metal cap. Eleanor unscrewed the metal cap, it was overly heavy for it's size. The other end cap was also removed and the same arrangement was in place. Two metal containers, bottom to bottom, covered in a custom made plastic casing complete with carrying handle. She knew when the containers were punctured and the components allowed to mix that the deadly gas would be released. From the size of this container and if used in a confined space, she thought, maybe hundreds of deaths. She held it up to the light.

'1020 carbon steel', said the man. 'Capable of withstanding the sarin I believe'.

'Yes. Remarkable, it's so small and well made', she mused.

'Progress Eleanor, progress. Now we want you to make the mixture tomorrow. When you have done this take it to the ladies toilet on floor two. Leave it in the first cubicle and walk away. Be there at three PM. Understood?'.

'You are mad', she began again 'I don't work with Sarin anymore, I'm now . . .'

'Enough', he bellowed, 'Enough, you are taking part in a Sarin trial tomorrow before lunch. I know this already, so no lies please. The equipment that you require will be there and available. If we do not have it by tomorrow night, I hope the God that you worship is kind to your brother'.

'Remember, ladies toilet, floor two, first cubicle'.

With that both men walked to the front hall, leaving Eleanor still sitting.

'Oh and Eleanor, no police. We will be watching', He said pausing at the door and turning his head. With that they were gone.

Eleanor broke down and for the first time in years she cried. A mixture of shock, anger and genuine concern for her brother had come to a head. The dam of emotions, normally so controlled and calm, had now overflowed. The banks were burst. She cried and cried.

CHAPTER 6

The Saab rolled along the main road, passing through Letterbrock village. The Navman, satellite navigation system hung on the black plastic arm at attached to the windscreen. The Abbot had driven all night and dawn was just beginning to break. 'Turn right in five hundred meters', said the well educated English woman's voice on the Sat-Nav. As the Abbot began his turn a Nissan X-Trail was almost at the junction travelling from the other direction. The Abbot braked sharply and readjusted his position on the road. The Nissan did not stop, pulling out at the mouth of the junction it turned left and sped away. Sitting stationary in the Saab the Abbot craned his neck trying to see a registration number or any identifiable markings on the jeep. As it was not fully daylight he saw nothing except that the vehicle had a yellow rear number plate, too dirty to get a registration number. He wondered why they were speeding off along this particular road. All his senses were now fully alert, as he drove slowly into the small side road.

The tyre noise had changed now from tarmacadam to gravel. Suddenly the English voice chirped up, 'Arriving at destination on left'. The abbot was startled for a second, then looking at the Sat-Nav he saw the chequered flag dancing on the small screen. A farmhouse and outbuildings were now coming up on the left. He slowed and glanced into the yard. A Toyota van and a BMW car sat nose to tail and a Mondeo was parked on their left close to the outbuilding. There were no people that he could see. The Saab rolled on picking up speed as it went, the road now turned a sharp almost ninety degree right, leading off into the mountain in the distance. Now approaching on the right was a small, newly planted forest. The local agricultural college rented this area and grew pine and fir trees of many different varieties, turning into the entrance he found the path into the forest blocked by a metal gate. The abbot turned the Saab, reversing into the entrance and stopping a few feet short of the metal barrier. Here his car was hidden from view of the farmhouse and its outbuildings. Killing the headlights and switching the engine off he reached into the driver's door pocket and drew out the Mauser 90 DA nine millimetre pistol. The Mauser was a copy of a Browning Hi-Power, made in the early nineteen nineties. It had been sitting there on a soft yellow cloth to prevent it sliding about when he was driving. He turned the pistol on it's side and pressed the magazine release catch. Sliding the magazine out he checked the brass bright rounds were in place. Full metal jacket rounds, then he pushed the magazine home and heard the metallic click as the magazine locked. Now grabbing the slide between his thumb and forefinger he crashed the slide to the rear, releasing it when it had travelled fully. It snapped forward collecting a round and chambering it. He pushed the safety catch off with his thumb and, leaning over on his left hip, he pushed the pistol into the covert trouser holster on his right buttock. The holster was inside his trousers and could not be seen when he stood up, only the belt clip was visible. The Mauser was ready now to draw and fire, seconds spent in preparation were seconds saved in combat. Lessons that had saved his life several times over.

The abbot opened the glove box and removed the second Mauser. It was wrapped in a leather and suede shoulder holster. The elastic straps coiled around the gun not wanting to give it up. He carefully unwrapped it, like a chef peeling a fruit, gently and deftly. Drawing the weapon he repeated the unloading process. This time, however, he put the full magazine into his left hand jacket pocket. Again from the glove box he produced a magazine full of the hollow point ammunition that he had bought on the Shankill Road. The rounds had the distinctive dome shaped sides but the top was flat. A hole drilled into the lead trapped the air as the round was fired. The projectile expanded on contact with skin, leaving horrific injuries. Hydrostatic shock was increased when these round struck human targets, the hollow lead centre was covered by a thin nickel jacket so that lead deposits would not be left in the barrel after firing. The abbot just liked the idea of them. Again the Mauser was made ready. He left the car quietly and shoved the pistol in his right hand jacket pocket, holding it by the butt, he walked off looking like a normal man with his hands in his jacket pockets this cold morning. Excitement and adrenaline coursed through him as he approached his target.

The abbot thought about the hollow point rounds and could feel his stomach turn over with excitement. Both the military and law enforcement were not allowed to use hollow point. Outlawed since the mid nineties and difficult to come by, he knew he was lucky. He felt like that wee boy on Christmas morning, unable to contain himself, wanting to take his new present out and play with it, endlessly.

Walking along the road he reached the blind corner and crossed straight away to the far side. Here he found a lower part in the dry stone wall and stepped through it dropping into the field. There was only one window in the farm house overlooking this field. As he approached the dwelling he drew out the Mauser from his jacket pocket. His thumb ran along the safety catch. Checking. Checking and re checking, it was off. The weapon was good. Ready to fire. He glanced in the dirty window as he passed. It was an old back room, a few chairs scattered here and there, newspapers and the general dross that a house collects when no one cares for it. At the corner he paused, looking around, before slipping toward the yard. His back gliding along the dwelling house wall, left hand outstretched feeling his way, like a blind man in an alley. At the second corner he could hear voices;

'Get out there and make sure'. One said.

'It's gotta be here some where'. This time a much deeper voice with a heavy southern Irish brogue.

The Abbot inched his way toward the open door. Scanning the yard all the while. It was empty, bereft of living things. No people, animals or birds. Empty. As he stepped in through the door he was confronted by a youth who had just turned to go out. The Abbot saw the M1 carbine the youth had in his left hand. His jaw dropped open as if to speak or was it surprise. The Abbot smashed the Mauser into his face in a vicious punch. The trigger guard broke the youths nose and sent him reeling backwards. Movement to his right made the Abbot spin around. A heavy set man in a white shirt was drawing a pistol from his waistband. Too slow. First shot was double action. The Mauser recoiled, the report was deafening in the farmhouse kitchen. With the Mauser now on single action two more rounds followed. Both chest shots. The man staggered and fell over the top of the body he had been searching. Red spots appearing on his white shirt. The Colt Python revolver slipped from his hands clattering onto the floor.

A second man appeared from the far side of the table, he was younger and very thin. He lunged over the table top toward the Abbot. His hands outstretched. Grabbing. Grabbing. He began to slide across the table. Almost touching the Abbot. The Mauser spoke once more. Blue spark. Yellow muzzle flash. The tinkle of the empty, ejected shell case as it ricochets off the draining board. The lifeless body slid along the table top and onto the floor. Arms still outstretched. A clean, neat head shot. Skull smashed into pieces as the hollow point found it's target and completed the job.

Turning now the Abbot surveyed the scene. Two other bodies lay on the floor. The bodies of the two he had just despatched lay half on top of them. The youth lay in the corner, blood gushing from his nose. Five people he thought. What is it with the number five? The youth stirred;

'Who are you?', asked the Abbot.

'Fuck off', spat the youth.

The Abbot scanned the kitchen area and had a quick look in both back rooms. Empty. As he returned he saw a set of secateurs on the kitchen windowsill. Someone must have loved the now overgrown garden at one time. Lifting them he walked over to the youth. Stooping he grabbed the M1 by the barrel and tossed it across the kitchen.

He returned the Mauser to his pocket and grabbed the youth by his left wrist, trailing him across the old wooden floor. He pulled the arm through between his legs, locking it in a vice like grip, twisting the wrist back against the joint. The youth howled in pain.

'Right', said the Abbot, 'question time. Don't fuck me about. Who are you?'.

'Fuck off', spat the youth again.

'Do you like nursery rhymes?' asked the Abbot.

Silence.

'This little piggy went to market . . .' he forced the youth's little finger into the secateurs and allowed it to bite slightly.

'Well, who are you?'

'Fuck you . . . .'

The blades nipped down, the youth squirmed and squealed. The Abbot cut and cut, twisting and nipping. A little finger fell to the floor. There was a torrent of blood everywhere.

'This little piggy stayed home . . . '.

'NO, NO more. I'm Real IRA and if you let me go we wont kill you . . . .'

'Did the piggy stay home? . . .

'What? . . .

The secateurs cut down again. This time the youth thrashed and punched at the Abbot with his free hand, but to no avail. Ring finger joined it's companion on the floor.

'I'm with the real IRA', screamed the youth, 'we were looking for a man . . .'

'What man?'

'I don't . . . I can't . . . .

'Roast beef', yelled the Abbot, moving the secateurs to the next finger.

'Well is it a roast beef dinner? . . .'

'No mister. No we were looking for a case. The dead man on the floor had it. Someone shot him before we got here . . . . please mister please . . .'

'What's in the case?'

'I don't . . . .'

'Dinner time . . . .' with that another finger joined the rest.

'Gas. Sarin gas. The muslim boys wanted it. We are helping them make a dirty bomb . . . . please that's all I know . . . .

The Abbot released the arm, at the same time drawing out the Mauser. The weapon spoke once more. Point blank this time. The lifeless body of the young man joined his lifeless fingers and his corpse colleagues on the kitchen floor.

Body searches were carried out on the men. Nothing. No clues. The mobile phone on the well dressed man rang when the Abbot dialled the number Mickey had given him. Going through his coat pockets a set of BMW keys were found. This man had been dead before the abbot arrived. Making his way to the car he searched it too. Inside the car, the boot compartment, even the engine bay. Nothing. Turning to walk away he thought about underneath the seats. Again nothing. Just before he stood up he noticed a small glove box to the right of the drivers steering wheel. Opening the door the Abbot removed a black plastic device, little bigger than a mobile telephone. The words on the front read Sat-Trak. Satellite Tracking system Fircove 500. Pushing the on button the sea green display informed him that it was locating satellites. Black bars with little numbers began to appear. Several minutes later the screen said 'Item sat-Trakked to lon 55' 22m n lat 27' 1mw. Co-ordinates thought the Abbot. With that he strolled away toward the old Saab. He could put these into his Satellite navigation system and hopefully locate the missing case.

As he replaced the pistols in the car he unloaded the hollow point magazine. Grinning he kissed the top round. Daddy loves his babies he said quietly and reached for the Sat-Nav System.

CHAPTER 7

Marc And Jay sat silently in the front of the big Nissan as it purred toward the town of Ballyclare. Marc kept glancing in the vanity mirror on the rear of his sun visor at their new addition as she dozed in the rear seat. She was early thirties and very tall and slim. She had blonde hair and brown eyes, which when they were closed displayed extremely long lashes. Her eyes opened as they neared their destination and Marc realised she was looking at him staring in the small mirror. His face flushed as he had been caught, she smiled at him and he noticed her whole face light up. His hand reached up and replaced the sun visor which snapped closed with a loud noise. Glancing over at Jay, Marc noticed he was smiling.

'Sun getting in your eyes Marc?' Laughed Jay.

'How far to the house?' asked Jenny.

'Ten more minutes'. Replied Jay and Marc together.

Neither of the two looked around but if they had they would have noticed Jenny's smile break into a broad grin.

The Nissan swung into the gravel drive and stopped in front of the double garage, at a large detached house in the Dale. This area was regarded as one of the better housing developments in Ballyclare.

'Very swanky'. Said a startled Jenny. 'I thought you CTO guys lived in flats and old warehouses and such'.

They all laughed. Marc opened the rear of the jeep and reached in to lift her bag. Jenny reached at the same time and both their hands touched as they grabbed the carrying handle together.

'It's OK, I got it', stammered Marc.

'Why thank you sir'.

'No problem. How long are you going to be with us?'

'I don't know. It will depend on what you recover and what state it is in.

Marc showed Jenny to her room and left her bag on the double bed. Jay had already gone to the shower and Marc was in the kitchen filling the kettle. A noise made him turn around and he saw Jenny standing in the doorway. Marc gave her a tour of the house and showed all the important things, the Bendix washing machine, the fridge and larder. The plasma television and DVD player, complete with a selection of DVD's and the remote controls for all. He opened the door into the double garage and Jenny followed him through. Mark walked to the tall, metal gun cabinet and turned to Jenny.

'This is where we keep the longs. Code is 9991, just punch it in if you need anything'.

'Longs?'

'Yeah. Long weapons. You know MP5's and the like'.

'Oh. Oh, I see. I don't, I mean I won't have a weapon'.

Marc looked puzzled.

'You don't carry. Not at all?'

'No Marc I don't, it's all scientific stuff with me. You shall have to protect me I'm afraid'

She stepped in close to Marc and looked directly at him. He gazed into her brown eyes and felt his face getting red again. Jenny smiled and Marc found himself smiling back.

'I'm sure Jay and I can look after you', he stammered.

'You got coffee in that kitchen?' she asked, turning away and walking back towards the door. Marc looked at her slender figure as she walked away. She was wearing a white T shirt with half sleeves and a pair of blue denim jeans. The jeans were cut tight to her legs and accentuated the curve of her hips and thighs. Marc stared and Jenny knew it. He followed her into the kitchen.

Both sat at the long pine table with a coffee on a wooden coaster in front of each. Marc's cup was a plain white beaker, he had given Jenny the pink cup with the yellow and blue flowers on it. It had been Emma's cup, she had brought it with her when she had first been assigned to the Dale. They were attempting to make small talk when Jay appeared in the doorway. He had a towel wrapped around him and was carrying the Bergen in his left hand and the H&K G3 in his right.

'Marc will you put the G3 away for me mate. I'm knackered and am gona get my head down before they ring with some other trauma?'

Marc arose and took the rifle, walking to the garage he opened the safe and deposited it. He returned and removed the rucksack from the kitchen. Jenny was gone. He spent several minutes sorting out the night sights and other equipment before placing it in the locked cupboards in the garage, just above the empty workbench. When he returned Jenny was back at the table with her laptop open and was tapping on the keys.

'So you are with the science division?' Marc asked.

'Oh yes. I'm at Porton Down. I take it you know why I'm here?'

'The Firm were not too specific but I take it we have lost something important?'

'Too right', laughed Jenny,' A whole flask of Sarin gas. Well to be specific two liquid components that when combined make up the gas'.

'Ooops', quipped Marc. 'And they think it's here?'

'I assume so, although my counterpart was flown to Scotland to the CTO guys there. So it looks as if they know it's missing, but aren't too sure exactly where it is'.

Marc watched her long slender fingers tap the keyboard. She was wearing glasses with thick brown frames and as she looked at Marc he could see her brown eyes. He felt a strong attraction to her and thought that a connection had been made when he touched her hand earlier. He wondered if she had noticed it too.

A stifled yawn signalled to Marc that bed was fast approaching. He excused himself and after a quick shower turned in. When he awoke it was late afternoon.

Marc dressed and hurried to the kitchen. The laptop was switched onto stand by but Jenny was not in the kitchen. Marc found her asleep on the sofa, the television on but the volume turned down. She awoke as he entered the room, and smiled at him.

'Good sleep?'

'Yes. I was tired'.

There was an awkward pause then Marc asked her;

'Would you like to eat out tonight. There is a good Chinese restaurant close by?'

'I'd love to'.

She sat up and again they exchanged glances.

'What time?'

'An hour or so?

'OK, I'll grab a quick shower'.

Marc telephoned the CTO base in London but there was no directive had been issued as to any follow up action. He was advised to stay close to the Dale and keep his mobile on. He intended to do that anyway. He rang off when he heard the bedroom door open and footsteps on the stairs.

Jenny appeared in the hall as Marc came out of the room. She was wearing a green and black dress and knee length black boots. She looked stunning. An emerald necklace and bracelet completed the outfit. Jenny was wearing very little makeup, just enough to enhance her already beautiful face and complexion. As she stooped forward to lift her small handbag Marc caught a glimpse of a green lace bra on delicate thin straps. His heart skipped a beat. She looked at him and smiled.

'This OK, not over dressed?'

'No, not at all. You look beautiful'. He had said it. He did not mean to say it aloud, but he had.

'Why, thank you sir', she quipped and her smile broadened into a grin. Marc was all but lost in her face.

Marc was wearing his jeans and an open neck shirt. He had his pistol with him as always, concealed in his waistband. A short, black leather jacket completed his simple outfit. He felt very plain and ordinary compared to her beauty.

In the restaurant they ate and talked. Marc, who was shy around women, felt completely at ease in her company. She told him that there had been a true love several years ago. He was a pilot in the RAF. The story unfolded that he had been sent to the first Gulf war and had been killed.

Not as a result of flying but in a car wreck. She said that something so simple had almost destroyed her.

Marc told her of his mother and father's death in a car crash and his education in Dublin afterwards. He spoke of his adoptive parents and grief and loneliness. She had made enquiries from a close friend in CTO's main office as to who was in the Ballyclare house in the Dale. The friend had spoken very highly of Marc and Jay. She liked Marc instantly and had not felt this way for quite a long time. Her friend had said that Marc was a heart throb with the girls in the Vauxhall office but had never asked any of them out. Now Jenny understood why, he was still grieving or at least he had been until tonight.

A bottle of red wine had been ordered and consumed with the meal. The restaurant was only a ten minute walk from the Dale and as they walked home Marc took her arm to help her across the road. His grip was delicate yet somehow familiar. Jenny knew that he had killed men in his job and was probably tougher than he looked. Jay had looked like a killer, all six foot four of him. He had big muscles and a great physique to match. He looked every inch a killer, yet Marc looked like an average man. Nothing about him made anyone pay him the slightest notice. Except Jenny, who thought he was very attractive and a gentleman also. As they crossed the road he dropped his hand from her arm. Their two hands brushed together. Jenny linked her arm through Marc's.

So they walked arm in arm, like teenage lovers, talking and putting the world to rights. It seemed that there was no subject they could not cover. Back at the house Marc again called CTO and they allowed him to stand down for the night. Jenny talked with him as they sat on the sofa. She had slipped her boots off and her long slender legs were draped over Marc's knee as the wrapped around each other like familiar lovers.

She had turned to face him, her cheek so close to his. Marc seized the moment and they kissed. It was tender, and loving. Filled with gentleness. Their lips brushed together and Marc's heart melted. Jenny was his and he knew it. Soon it was late and time for bed. They kissed again at her bedroom door. She whispered goodnight and softly closed the bedroom door. She stood with her back to the door when she entered the room. She listened as Marc closed his door and went to bed. Jenny lay awake on top of her bed. She had taken her dress off and was wearing her matching bra and pants. She knew sleep would not come.

In his room Marc too lay on top of his bed clothes. His mind was racing at a thousand miles an hour. She was just the most beautiful girl he had ever seen and he felt so easy in her company. After a time he decided to get up, sleep would not be his tonight. The combination of an earlier sleep, the wine and meeting Jenny was too much. As he opened his bedroom door to go downstairs he found Jenny standing in her open doorway. Framed in the streetlight, making her outline definite and feminine. Marc grabbed for her and they kissed, this time with an urgency. His tongue probed her delicate mouth, he could taste her lipstick. She yielded straight away and both fell backwards onto the bed. He kissed her neck and held her tighter than she had ever remembered. His hand released her green, lace bra and it was pulled off. Marc discarded it on the bedroom floor. Jenny's small round breasts now pushed into Marc's chest, he felt her pink nipples harden as they touched. His hand grabbed for them, but Jenny caught it and held it onto her breast. She moaned, a low, delicious noise. Marc pulled his face away and gazed at her. At last she was his, they both knew it.

More kisses followed and Jenny rolled over pushing her back into Marc. She pulled her knees up and her matching, green lace pants quickly followed the bra onto the bedroom floor. Marc held her gently by the throat as she pushed back hard against him. Her hand found its way to Marc and she guided him inside. The act was deliberate, yet gently executed. She fell into the rhythm of his pounding body, she was lost for a short while, he pulled her head back and they kissed again. Then he slipped out and rolled onto his back. Jenny deftly straddled him and this time he needed no guiding. He drove into her, his hands behind her knees, pushing them wide. She sat upright taking him deeper and deeper inside. At last she moaned and her limbs went rigid. Then she fell forward like a rag doll, smothering him with kisses.

Marc carried on, still with that gentle urgency, she again rose and fell on top of him as a second wave erupted over her. She let out a long moan before rolling off him and onto the bed. This time there were cuddles and stroking. Never before had that been the case. Sure sex had been good with her boyfriends, but never this level of care taken or tenderness shown. This was something new, something very special. This was different and she loved it.

After a short while Marc began to kiss her again. He was insatiable and she was loving all the attention. He pulled her close to him and mounted her. Again the lovemaking continued and again she synchronised with him. He was pushing and she was resisting in just the right quantity. He bent forward and whispered into her ear;

'Jenny, I love you'.

'I know and I'm so glad'.

They wrapped the bed sheet around them when lovemaking was over. Both were pulled tightly together. Even their breathing while asleep fell into a perfect rhythm. Jenny fell asleep listening to the sound of Marc's heart gently beating. In her subconscious she was back in the womb, all safe and warm and protected. They slept the sleep of love that knows no distance or bounds. Total, peaceful sleep. Perfect in it's simplicity.

CHAPTER 8

It was a Saturday morning, like so many others in the village of Winterborne Gunner. Ian Mckeller, the village postman stopped at the gate of the red brick cottage. He held three letters for a Miss Eleanor Clarke in his left hand and scanned the envelopes to ensure that there was no crease or tear or wrinkle that she may complain about. She complained a lot, a well written letter to the postmaster general had landed Ian with a severe reprimand. This was later withdrawn when a series of letters of complaint, each one more bizarre than the last were received. Some were simple 'the gate was not properly closed' letters others were 'he is scruffy and disheveled' type. Either way all the other postmen had refused to deliver her mail as a result. So Ian was left to carry on. He opened the small gate and walked up the path. The letters were dropped through the letterbox as requested in her last letter. There was a box on the outside wall but it appeared that the rain leaked in and the mail was wet. Of course this was automatically Ian's fault. He noticed the milk not yet lifted in from the doorstep. That's odd, he thought and if it were any of the other houses he would have investigated further. Not so with Miss Clarke. Milk on doorstep is milk on doorstep he mused.

On Friday afternoon, Eleanor had completed the Sarin Gas test that had been scheduled. All morning she could not get the images of her brother and his family out of her head. She had taken the flask into her work inside her large brown handbag. Although she should have been searched the security men were afraid of her and she very often only received little more than a cursory glance. Eleanor would often complain about the officers who exceeded their tea break times or had too many toilet breaks. So no one noticed the flask in the brown leather handbag. The same could be said regarding the laboratory and it's running procedures. The rest of the scientists were in teams, not so Eleanor. She did her own thing, so to speak, while at work. The filling of the flask was carried out as she had been requested to do by her visitors and when completed it was secreted in her handbag again. A quick trip to the toilet at the allotted time and the flask was left where she had been instructed to leave it.

At four twenty Eleanor returned to the toilet, but found the flask gone. She left work at her normal time and cycled home.

No milk or letters were delivered on Sunday.

Monday morning arrived and a startled milkman found two unopened pints on the doorstep. He should have investigated further but had no wish for any further complaints. He left the fresh new bottle of milk and walked away. It had been a while since she had written to his supervisor in the dairy informing them of the 'awful, tuneless, whistling noise she was forced to endure every morning'. The tuneless whistler walked back to his milk float and moved onto the next dwelling.

Eleanor's work colleagues noticed her missing and eventually someone checked the Annual Leave board. She was not listed. No one really wanted to grasp the nettle.

Don Metcalfe, her immediate supervisor telephoned her and left an answer phone message.

At twelve minutes past twelve Don Metcalfe was summoned to the director general's office. This was very unusual and a somewhat startled Don found the Director with two tall men in their early thirties wearing ill fitting dark lounge suits. As he entered the office he caught the end of a somewhat heated discussion. Everyone turned to look at him.

CHAPTER 9

Marc staggered his way down the stairs into the kitchen. It was just before nine am. The noise of the back door closing had awakened him, leaving Jenny asleep, he decided to make breakfast. In the kitchen he was confronted by Jay wearing his jogging bottoms and vest top.

'Hi jay. Going running?'

Jay turned to look at Marc, he was wearing the biggest grin Marc had ever seen.

'Just back mate. Did about four miles but the weather's shit'.

Marc gazed at the window and saw the rain streaming down the pane, he could hear the wind had fairly increased since his stroll home last night.

'Jenny still asleep?'

'Yeah, Jay. I think so'

'You think so do you? I think you should have closed her bedroom door last night', sniggered Jay. Marc felt his face flush, again and looking at Jay he said:

'Aw I suppose I should have'.

'Taking her up breakfast then?'

'Yeah, scrambled eggs and toast. Want some?'

'Too right. I'll grab a quick shower first though'.

Marc cooked with all the finesse of a single man who had lived alone for a very long time. When his masterpiece was created the kitchen looked as if a hand grenade had exploded on the work top. Egg shells, spilled milk, butter cartons and all the pans and plates associated with the experience lay strewn on the bench. He plated Jay's and set it on the table with a mug of tea. The dainty plate and cup were placed on the round plastic tray and he deftly carried them upstairs. Jay was on the landing and said nothing but grinned at Marc again. Marc wished he would find another topic to laugh at. Jay cantered downstairs and at the bottom burst into the lyrics of a Queen song. Lover boy. Marc shook his head and opened the room door.

Jenny was sitting up in the bed and smiled as Marc entered.

'Ah, is this room service then?' she whispered

'Why yes madam, would you like me to turn down your sheets?'

She smiled again. She absolutely beamed. Marc could feel the whole mood and room liven up. It was a fantastic atmosphere. Electric almost.

He sat down on the end of the bed and set the tray down between them. Both ate and talked with the same ease as last night. The conversation was old and comfortable and both again felt like lovers in a much longer relationship. Marc collected the debris on the tray and returned to the kitchen. A short while later Jenny joined Marc and Jay at the table. She was wearing her jeans and a pink sweater which accentuated her shapely figure. Opening up her laptop she tapped the keys.

Marc shot a glance at Jay who was smiling back. If Jenny saw it she made no comment nor paid it any attention. Marc's Blackberry rang and disturbed the peace.

'Hi'.

'Mr Marc?'

'Yep'.

'It's Mr Christian. Can you talk'.

'Yes go ahead'.

'We can confirm that a canister of Sarin Gas is missing from Porton. Exact amount not known at the moment but enough to cause concern. The science officer with you can brief Jay and yourself shortly. I've sent her an E mail outlining what we know.'

'Do you think it is in Northern Ireland?'

'Almost certainly. The two DNA samples you sent us have been identified. I'm sending you a secure Brent Fax as we speak. One is a PIRA chap. We think that a dirty bomb is being constructed over there but for a mainland or European target'.

'OK. What instructions have you?'

'Sit tight at the minute. We will contact as soon as it changes or we know more.'

Marc relayed the message to his two colleagues, then switched the Brent phone, located underneath the stairs, to fax mode. Several seconds later four pages came pouring out of the large secure printer attached to the phone. The Brent was a very old system. It was, however, the only foolproof system that the British had used to date. The phone line was separate. There were three filters on each end of the line and a de-coder and en-coder built into the phone. There was a slight delay when speaking on the telephone handset but it was rarely used. The fax system was frequently used. Marc gathered up the thin fax paper and carried it to the table.

Jenny had finished with her Emails and computer when Marc returned. She smiled at him and said:

'You two ready for an update then?'

'Go for it', beamed Jay.

'Right. The Sarin Gas is missing from Porton Down, so therefore it is military spec and not some unknown or home made type. So we can deduce it will be full strength. It is normally transported in liquid form, by isolating the two liquids that when combined make the gas. The detonation of a small explosion in the right circumstances, or as we call it a binary bomb, will produce the gas and the after spread. All good so far?'

Both men nodded. They had a limited knowledge of such items but were lacking in the specifics.

'The gas will be used in a confined area, like a tube station or shopping centre. Somewhere where it can cause maximum effect. It won't kill very many people as it will be in a small quantity but the after spread will be catastrophic'.

'Explain that', asked Jay 'the after spread?'

'Yeah. Imagine if it was a small bomb at say a football match. Hidden in the grounds of Old Trafford or some such. A massive car bomb could kill hundreds. But a dirty bomb may only kill ten or twenty. The after effects though would cripple everyone. Firstly no one would be allowed to leave the grounds. Police in NBC suits, with guns, would have to seal the area. Hospital A&E units having to prepare contamination suites everywhere, at the scene and again at the hospital. Family members arriving at the grounds to find relatives and not being allowed in, supporters wanting out of the grounds and being held against their will by armed police. Soldiers or police having to shoot anyone crossing the contamination line in case it is more than Sarin gas involved in the dirty bomb. Street disorder and riots will ensue as people try to free the victims from the stadium. There is also the fact that all football grounds would all have to close to review security. The loss of billions of pounds in revenue, clubs having to close permanently. The effects are far reaching and will last for years and years'.

'Not just football though', interjected Marc, 'shopping centres or public buildings or transport systems. It could be any of these'.

'Oh yes Marc. It is a great weapon to cause terror. That is what it is for, extreme terror for the public and the government too'.

'Does it kill immediately?' asked Marc.

'Well the people exposed to it, who have not been killed in the bomb blast, will die as soon as they breathe it in. It's a terrible death. Choking and convulsing, it attacks the nervous system. Others slightly further away will show breathing difficulties almost at once. The further away from the gas the milder the symptoms. Many will die in the first twenty four hours and so on. The media will have a field day when they research this and will assist in the spreading of panic. Facebook and twitter updates and u tube uploads will spread the panic in no time firstly nation wide then on a global scale as victims and people at the scene try to communicate with loved ones. Yeah a brilliant weapon for the terrorists'.

'We don't have enough armed police', interjected Jay, 'I mean there are a few armed response units scattered across the country. The police could not contain the scene for more than a few hours'.

'That's why the PSNI here in Northern Ireland have been training Tactical Support Units in NBC and chemical counter measures. The units here can be mobilised and flown to the mainland at a few hours notice. All are armed and trained in the use of firearms and have worked with the British military for a very long time. So they are the perfect choice'.

'This has already been thought out?' asked Marc

'And planned for?' chimed Jay.

'Oh yes, quite a while ago'. Confirmed Jenny.

Jenny had been flown to Steeple Barracks near Antrim where she was involved in the initial setting up of the NBC training. She was one of three scientists who delivered talks and gave pointers to the Combined Operational Trainers within the PSNI. Her speciality was gas delivery and effects. The other scientists talked of Anthrax and other various chemical agents used in biological warfare. Suits had been provided for all TSG members. One was to be used for training and one was the suit to be kept for the real thing. They all hoped that they would never be needed, but man has never developed a weapon that has remained unused. So with that in mind it is really only a matter of time.

The NBC suits came in dark red carrier bags and each has the police number of the officer attached to its carrying handle. There were also gas masks and detachable canisters with special filters included in the kit. Radiation detectors and a plethora of other equipment is available and the officers are trained in it's use. The PSNI remain the perfect choice for this type of operation.

CHAPTER 10

Marc and Jay had listened intently to Jenny's briefing and were now reading some small Aide-Memoire type publications that were obviously issued to the military and police.

Marc gathered up the fax messages sent earlier by Mr Christian. He placed two on the table, they contained photographs of the men Jay and he had found shot dead at the farmhouse.

'Right this man', he held up a picture,'Is Benjamin Pious Macnamara, fifty nine years of age, has been training PIRA in small arms for over forty years. Served in Irish Army for a spell. Never been arrested, never been in gaol, no relatives remaining. He has a variety of associates, all PIRA/INLA, many dead or serving time either on mainland, or Northern and Southern Ireland. It says here he has not been thought to have been on any combative operations. Just a weapons instructor. Cause of death is multiple gunshots'.

'Multiple gunshots, no shit Sherlock', quipped Jay dryly.

'Second man', said Marc holding up the second picture,' Is one Desmond Murphy, 48 years old, lives in Maghera in Northern Ireland but has recently been in the Middle East on business. Says he's an import export consultant and has several trucks and vans on the road. Mostly in Southern

Ireland. Runs a parcel distribution network. Had been on the Dublin Liverpool boat that day and had driven to Letterbrock as soon as it docked. Death by, wait for it Jay, multiple gunshots'.

'Any terrorist connections?' asked Jay

'Doesn't say. He must have had some, otherwise why would he be in Letterbrock?'

'Visiting a friend, doing a favour?' asked Jenny.

Both men looked at her and she smiled again.

'Just a thought', she added.

The Saab rolled into Fivemilletown with the Abbot at the wheel. He was driving with one hand and looking at the satellite tracking device with the other. The sat-nav told him he was arriving at his destination on the left. As he cruised the one way system he passed the Golden Wok, Chinese takeaway. It was the only building located on that side and was closed. There was a large car park just beyond it and a number of trucks and articulated trailers were parked up there. The Abbot joined them. Reversing the Saab in between the trailers and almost out of sight. The tracking device had changed as he passed the take away. He noticed the green light had turned red and began to flash. The Abbot reckoned that the merchandise must be very close. Switching off the sat nav he got out of the vehicle after going through the Mauser pistol ritual again. So with one tucked into his jeans and one in his jacket pocket he approached the take away on foot.

Walking past it he noticed that the front window had a wire mesh grille attached. The door was covered by a pull down metal shutter. The building had a yard at the side with a high concrete wall around it. There was a corrugated metal gate with a rough chain looped through it. Although hidden from view he guessed that there was a substantial padlock to go with the chain. He did not stop or try to look through the holes in the gate. Instead he noticed a church within walking distance, it was being refurbished and had a scaffold erected on one side. That should allow me the vantage point I need, he mused.

A few minutes later he was half way up the scaffold. Standing on a wooden landing where one ladder finished and another began. He could hear the workmen far above him, yet no one had challenged him or even noticed him. This high vantage point afforded a grand view of the rear of the take away. There was a black four by four parked in the yard. It had the classic blackened windows and looked like a pimp or drug dealers car. It made The Abbot smile. Why do people feel the need to do that he wondered. It's like the skinhead and hard dogs thing. Why did skinheads feel the need to shave their hair off and why do these tattooed half brains always buy muscle dogs like pitbull terriers? It made the Abbot laugh. Anyway, there were two quad bikes in the yard and some sort of long, galvanised trailer, possibly for the bikes. A power washer and several brushes were also strewn around the yard. There were two Chinese men, late teens or early twenties, in the yard. As the Abbot watched a window of opportunity began to open for him.

The F6 Volvo, rigid liquid petroleum gas truck pulled up at the take away gate and a driver in a blue coveralls, wearing a baseball cap climbed out. He spoke with one of the youths and the returned to his cab. There was the sound of chain running through metal and the men opened the yard gate. The Volvo truck pulled forward, blocking the road and then began to reverse into the yard. The Abbot could hear the reversing buzzer and see the hazard warning lights on the truck flashing. Wasting no time he rapidly climbed down the ladder and walked to the restaurant. His right hand went inside his jacket and he felt the warm, wooden covered butt of his friend. Thumb ran along the slide snicking the safety off. Fingers gently caressing the metal as his gun foreplay began.

At the gate he paused and then glanced inside. The truck was blocking the gateway. The driver and one of the Chinese youths were at the rear working with the bulk liquid gas tank. He could hear the metallic scrapings and the clinking noise of the almost empty vessel. Slipping past them, past the front of the truck he stepped into the yard proper. His hand drew out the pistol, no need to glance at it. He knew, he felt it's presence. Old familiar. Death deliverer. Stepping inside the store room at the rear of the takeaway he saw a table in the centre of the room. There were upright freezers and coolers of all descriptions along the walls. A dozen bags of potatoes and vegetables were stacked behind the only door which must have led into the take away kitchen. He could hear voices coming from the kitchen. An electric kettle was boiling water on a small worktop just the far side of the door.

On the table lay four H&K MP5 sub machine pistols. They had been stripped down and were now a pile of springs, barrels, triggers and plastic guards. A tin of penetrating oil spray, cloths and cleaning rods lay amongst them. Magazines and ammunition were stacked on a chair sitting beside the table. The MP5's were in the process of being cleaned. Obviously they had been used recently as there was a lot of carbon and cordite residue all over the table top. That's when he saw it. An aluminium photographers case. He knew instantly. Bringing the tracker from his pocket he saw the light was now a steady red. This was it. The case was sitting near the door, on an empty, uncluttered bit of worktop. A cordless drill and a selection of drill bits lay beside it. The combination lock on the case had been drilled and as he stepped closer he could see the innards of the lock mechanism in pieces on the bench. Replacing the Mauser in his pocket he deftly lifted and opened the case. Inside it was packed with foam and a black flask was secured in the foam casing. A quick examination told him that there was no place for a tracker on the flask. So the tracker transmitter had to be in the foam packing. Good. He removed the flask and closed the case replacing it on the bench. He was retracing his steps when the kettle clicked off with a loud snap. Whang Lee spun around in his kitchen and looked at the kettle in his store. Boiled and about time. He shouted to the rest of them in his native tongue that coffee was ready. There would be time for a few games of cards too, before opening. Stepping out into the store he glanced to the bench. The case was still there, guns still on the table. He lifted the kettle and returned to his kitchen, unaware that one second earlier he would most certainly have been gunned down. No coffee, no cards. That is how fickle life can sometimes be. He made the coffee, also unaware that in a very few hours he would be pleading for his life and watching his friends lose theirs as a punishment for their incompetence.

The Abbot slipped past the front of the gas lorry and turned up the street. A few minutes later the Saab rolled out of the car park and took the main Belfast Road.

CHAPTER 11

Don Metcalfe had taken the news very badly. A hammer blow if ever he had felt one. The Director and his two friends, from the security services, had been accusing his department of being careless in the extreme. They said that Sarin Gas had possibly been removed from the laboratory. From his laboratory, under his control? No way, he had told them. He tried to explain how difficult the gas is to transport. Tried to explain the level of knowledge required and finally the fact that armed security men, not to mention MOD policemen were in place to stop such an outrage.

All to no avail. Six eyes looked accusingly at him. What would the security services know about sarin? What would they know of the dedication of Eleanor Clarke and people like her? He agreed to find her and speak with her immediately. The Director said he had phoned the MOD police who would accompany him to her house and bring her back to Porton Down where the matter could be resolved. Don left the office feeling upset and annoyed that the Director had taken the word of two unknowns against that of one of his most senior staff.

In the foyer Don met with a very young, slim policeman. He was wearing the blue NATO pullover and blue canvas trousers of his office. A light blue shirt and black tie completed the outfit. He wore a dark blue cap and all looked very co-ordinated and matching except for the large khaki webbed belt with the brass clip and the long khaki webbed holster slung at an acute angle around his waist. A heavy Browning nine millimetre pistol nested inside the holster and a green, thick lanyard came from the pistol butt coiling up around the officers shoulder.

'Mr Metcalf, I'm P.C. Brown', began the young man.

Don smiled. 'You got a first name?'

'Sorry, it's Eric. Eric Brown'.

'Are we going in my car?'

'No sir, I have the police landrover outside. My instructions are to take you but I can follow you if you like?'

'No, that's fine. I will let you drive. You know Winterbourne Gunner and Miss Clarkes address?'

'Yes. I know the house'.

Both men left the foyer and walked the short distance to the staff car park where a dark blue Landrover 110 Defender awaited. Don pulled open the passenger door and climbed onto the grey plastic seat. He closed the door and was startled by how light it was. Aluminium, he told himself. Unsure he reopened the door and closed it again. The dash board was sparse and a police radio sat on the small ledge just behind the window and above the air vents fitted by Landrover. The radio had been fitted by someone with a love of coarse work and self tapping screw nails. A black metal bracket had been screwed to the plastic dash and the radio hastily fitted to it. The microphone had no securing point, although there were two small holes where the chrome clip had once been fitted. Now, missing, the handset dangled on the curly, coiled rubber covered wire. It swung violently to and fro as the vehicle lurched along the car park and out onto the concrete lane that led to the main gate.

A short while later both men were sitting in the Landrover outside Eleanor Clark's cottage. Don Metcalf climbed out and followed the officer to her front door. He began knocking loudly and after several minutes he opened the letter box and looked inside. Both men exchanged glances. Don walked around to the side door, the one Eleanor had used most of the time. He remembered visiting her on a few occasions and once had stayed for a coffee. It was just that he remembered. A coffee. No biscuits or buns. Not even sugar, just coffee. She is indeed a strange lady he mused. As he rounded the corner at the edge of the house he noticed her bicycle in it's mini car port. It was padlocked. The side door was locked.

'I'm going to smash the window', said PC Brown.

'Why?' asked Don. 'It's a normal door lock not a Yale type. So even if you can turn the handle from the inside it still won't open'.

The policeman stooped and looked through the keyhole. Clear. Empty. No key in the lock, he was right. He felt foolish.

'So what do you suggest?'

Don moved past the door and around the rear of the house. The downstairs bathroom window was slightly ajar. The window was small but Don thought that the slim officer might just fit through.

'Here. Can you get in there?'

PC Brown nodded. He unclipped his belt and lanyard and handed it to Don. Again Don was surprised at the heavy weight of the belt and pistol. His NATO pullover and clip on tie came off too. Unsure about the pistol he looked at Don.

'Don't take the pistol out sir', he said, 'maybe I'd best unload it'.

'Look', said Don, 'Just climb through the bloody window and open the front door'.

The officer turned away like a scolded schoolboy and began the arduous climb. First onto the bin then the window sill, green with moss. He pulled the top opening window as far up as he could. His head and shoulders disappeared through the opening. He was shouting,'Don't worry Miss Clarke, police here coming in'. He repeated several variations of this chant to hide his nerves. He was concerned what awaited him inside. As Don had mentally predicted there was an almighty crash as the officer knocked some items off the windowsill on the inside and they fell into the wash basin. The officer's feet, now at a very acute angle then disappeared all at once. It looked as if the window had eaten him. Swallowed him whole. Silence followed. Don retraced his steps and went back to the front door. He felt rather foolish standing there holding a pistol in a canvas holster.

Eric Brown had only served three years in the MOD police. He now found himself in one of those situations that they cannot train you for. He had peeped inside the bathroom window. There was a musty, damp smell. The smell of lavender too. Faint and dainty but still detectable. He managed to squeeze his arms through and then balance his midriff on the window bar. His long arms reached down and grabbed the sides of the wash basin. As he pulled himself in through the window his elbow brushed against something and the electric toothbrush and it's pink plastic holder spun off the sill. The holder crashed into the sink, the brush smashed on the hard tiled floor, spewing out batteries and wires and pieces of broken plastic. Oh shit. Now I'm for it, he thought.

Eric reached that critical stage as he pulled himself in through the window. That stage where the point of balance shifts. It can sometimes shift rapidly and did so in Eric's case. His arms were not able to stop the downward landslide of body mass and he soon followed the toothbrush. Managing to mostly miss the wash basin he ended up in a heap on the floor. Getting to his feet he suddenly felt very much in the lion's den. He could hear his heart thumping and found he was sweating. Get a grip, he told himself. It was to no avail. He knew. He could feel it. Something was wrong. Very wrong.

He walked out of the bathroom and found he was looking down the hallway toward the front door. He marched toward it. The open door to the back room awaited him. He walked briskly past. Don't look in he told himself. Too late. From the corner of his eye he saw it. Grotesque, horrible, the stuff of hellish nightmares. He slowly looked to his right. Eleanor sat bolt upright in her high backed wing chair. She was wearing a green cardigan and a long blue denim skirt. Her hands were gripping the arm rests. Her head. Well, that was the story. Her head was inside a clear, heavy plastic bag. Her face appeared to have a bluish colour and her tongue protruded from her mouth. It was black as coal and swollen. The inside of the bag stuck to her face. But it was her eyes. Staring. Silently accusing him of entering her lair. Glazed, open, dead eyes. He bolted toward the front door. The key was sticking in the lock. The door was heavy and had no window. He pulled it open so violently that Don jumped back. Eric vomited at Don's feet, running to the grass he gagged and shook uncontrollably. Don entered the house and returned a few minutes later. He was on his mobile phone. His office were contacting the local police. He walked to the Landrover and opened the door. Inside he found a roll of police blue and white tape which had MOD POLICE emblazoned on it. Walking back to the house he reached it to Eric.

'Here son, the real police will be here shortly. Best get this around the house and gate. Eh lad?'

Eric smiled and thanked him. Replacing his gunbelt he began to unfurl the tape. He had a feeling his already long day had just become longer.

CHAPTER 12

Jamal Kharim had worked for Cleanwell Industrial cleaners for three years now. His daily grind were the three back buildings at Porton down, military research establishment. Two of the buildings contained classrooms and equipment stores, so he had access to all areas. However, the third building, well that was another matter. He had only access to the first and second floor toilet areas. Each day he would make three trips to them. One at eight am, when he started, one at eleven thirty am and the last one at three ten pm. His pass only opened the small side door and allowed access to the male toilets on the ground floor and the female ones on the second. All other doors had electronic locks. The corridors were covered at every angle by cameras and there were metal shutters beside all the fire doors. Once during a fire drill rehearsal he had observed these doors closing automatically. They were operated from the main command room located across the yard. Jamal did not know if they assisted the fire doors or replaced them of if they were to contain people as well as fire. He just knew that if he was suspected or caught the doors would activate and he would be like the proverbial rat in a trap. Not an idea that he relished.

Jamal had been in England for seven years and had held several jobs in that time. He was a qualified motor vehicle mechanic and had worked in two garages in London. Four years ago at his local Mosque he was approached by an old friend. Jamal agreed to attend evening classes in the Mosque and found himself a willing recruit for the oncoming Jihad. His English work colleagues were coarse talking and ignorant to the plight of others around the world. They drank lots, read filthy newspapers and referred to him as Vindaloo or Gupta. Their day was consumed by talk of football players and up and coming games. They were proud whenever a player would be caught in a brothel or wreck a super car in some drunken accident. They delighted in reading of their sexual exploits and often talked as if they were talented players and what they would do and how they would live life. It almost always involved women, drugs and drinking. Jamal had grown to hate them.

Three years ago he was given the cleaners job. The company was owned by another man who prayed at his Mosque and attended the evening classed. He had just landed a military contract. The pay was a lot less than Jamal was already getting but he agreed to take the cleaning job anyway. A few weeks after he began his new job, envelopes started arriving at his house. One per week. They contained cash, the money was the difference in the wages he had just lost. Allah had indeed smiled upon him.

Now, today, was his time. It was three pm and he walked quickly to the third building. Building number 221. He had his yellow plastic mop bucket with him, carrying it by the handle. The plastic handled mop sticking out of the bucket and held in place and upright by his long fingers. The bucket had an aluminium base clipped onto it with four large rubber wheels attached. He set the bucket down and ran his ID card through the metal lock keeper.

The light on the door lock flashed green and he was in. In the cleaners store he filled the bucket with water and at three pm he entered the Gents toilets.

Several minutes later he knocked the door of the female toilets and pushing it ajar called out. All was quiet. He slipped inside. In the second cubicle he found the black flask, sitting on the floor as he had been told. Lifting it he dropped it into the mop bucket, after a quick wash of the floor and the signing of the job sheet on the back of the door, he slipped out. At the cleaners store on the ground floor he tipped out the water but made sure the flask remained. The flask was covered by the mop head and at a quick glance could not be easily noticed.

Back at the main building, where the cleaners store incorporated changing rooms, clothes lockers and showers, he stashed his mop bucket upside down on the metal draining grille after he had removed his prize. The heavy black plastic flask was placed inside his navy blue holdall beside his metal lunch box. Some clothes were scattered on top. He knew that his bag would be looked in by the security guards. It always was. In fact in this whole plan this was the biggest and most likely threat. He would deny it. Just before he left the changing room he uttered a prayer under his breath. A short prayer. Just one, small request.

Feeling a surge of inner strength, Jamal lifted his bag and walked to the main building. As he rounded the corner at the main door he found himself in the centre of a group of builders. There must be twelve or thirteen, he thought. They were working on a new building up at the armoury complex. Their passes had the large red X on them, meaning they were workmen on contract and only cleared for outside areas. His pass, on the other hand was blue and had his photograph and details on it. A yellow

J below his photograph meant cleaning staff/restricted access. Jamal joined the queue. Three security guards were at the desk, the end guard glanced at jamal's pass and motioned for him to come forward to his station. Jamal was sweating and trying to avoid eye contact. Setting the holdall up on the desk he removed the pass and handed it to the guard. No one spoke. The guard hovered for a few seconds, which seemed like an age to Jamal. What would he say? What would Jamal tell him? Would they torture him when they discovered? This was a bad plan. A very ill thought out plan. No plan at all in fact.

The guard turned away and hung Jamal's pass on the board behind him. He lifted down Jamal's other identity card and reached it to him. It allowed him access through the main gates both entering and leaving. He smiled at Jamal and bid him good afternoon. Jamal nodded, lifted his still unopened bag and walked out without looking back. After a few minutes walk he had reached the main gate. Holding his pass up to the mirror glass at the main security hut he saw his reflection. He looked gaunt and tired. He was still sweating. The gate buzzer sounded signalling the pedestrian gate was open. Jamal pulled the metal handle and stepped out of Porton Down and onto the main road. At the bus stop a short walk away he began to shake. His mouth was dry and he felt sick and light headed. Allah had indeed smiled upon him. Allah be praised, there is no god but Allah, he told himself.

CHAPTER 13

Desmond Murphy had stopped at the Weston services in Salisbury and was filling up his five series, diesel BMW. He covered many thousands of miles in the course of a year, his work taking him all over England and sometimes Europe. Having built a good transport and distribution business would have been enough for most men, but Desmond. Well, he liked the idea of striving to get more. Always, he needed more. Never satisfied with his lot. He had just purchased two new Scania trucks from the main dealer in Penrith, Cumbria. He liked dealing face to face as it where, like his father when he was horse trading and it had paid off. No reduction on the purchase price but a free years vehicle servicing thrown in when he threatened to take his money elsewhere. Oh, and a free lunch. Desmond like that idea. Free lunch was always good.

The fuel pump snapped shut and Desmond parked the BMW just off the forecourt and went to pay in the garage shop. He had left his vehicle unlocked as he had been instructed via the text message. In the shop he purchased a cup of cappuccino and a paper. Sitting down by the window he could see the car. Desmond waited the ten minutes the message had instructed him to before returning to his car. As he climbed in he noticed the aluminium photographers case sitting on the passengers seat. It made him smile, even though he had been watching his

BMW for the majority of the time, someone had opened it and left the case. He admired professionals no matter what their chosen occupation.

Although his family were from a strongly republican area Desmond had never worked for the PIRA or CIRA or anyone. He had been approached on a number of occasions and had always donated cash, but declined the work opportunities. He knew some of his drivers had in the past, and he turned a blind eye. This time, however, it had been very different. For one thing he had made many friends in the Middle East as he had established an import business last year. The second thing was the money. Well, with the global recession in full swing money was money and this was worth millions. It made him smile, he liked money, lots of money.

He opened the case and found the envelope inside as promised. Reading the instructions he pulled the small tracking device out of the foam lining and switched it on. After a few seconds it paired with the case transmitter. Switching off the device he concealed it in a small glove box just underneath the steering wheel. His BMW had several storage areas but this one was well hidden. Desmond wondered why the Germans had located it there and what items other drivers placed in it. He thought that most car owners would not even be aware of it's existence. He pulled out his road map as he had been instructed not to use a sat-nav on this mission. That made him smile too, all this cloak and dagger stuff. James Bond eat your heart out. Studying the Collins road map he quickly found the A338 and began his journey.

A short while later he passed the bus stop close to the main gate at Porton Down. He pulled over into the lay-by just past the bus stop. As he pulled in he noticed as Asian man standing alone, holding a gripper bag. Desmond rolled the window down as per his text message instructions. The man stepped forward and reached into his bag, pulling out a black flask. Then stooping he said;

'Twenty?'.

'Six', replied Desmond, feeling even more James bond than before.

The black flask was dropped into the seat and the man turned and was gone in seconds. Desmond drove off. Looking in his mirror he saw the man waiting at the bus stop. Desmond dialled the number pre—programmed into the mobile he had been given. The instructions were very clear. Place the flask in the aluminium case, scatter the combination numbers and drive to the Liverpool boat. He pulled over a short distance away and did as he had been asked. Next stop Liverpool he thought.

The main offices of CTO were busy with all the data and intelligence reports regarding the missing gas from Porton down. Everyone was keen to get a lead or any clue as to the whereabouts of the poison. The British press had been served with a D notice, forbidding any release on this item. The Irish press were being contacted also and the Home Office were looking at the situation with growing concern. The Prime Minister had been informed and an emergency meeting of the Cabinet had been called for that very evening. However, at the minute it was still a best guess scenario. In Belfast the Chief constable of the PSNI had been contacted and asked to place three hundred officers on standby. PSNI headquarters at Knock in Belfast were buzzing as the emergency planning office moved up a gear. Two disused command rooms were re opened and computers booted up and ready to roll by

0900 hours the next morning. All in all the behind the scenes work was falling into place. Everyone was told that it was a routine operation and a test of readiness, but the Chief constables officers were not so sure.

In Holywood the MI5 base at Palace Barracks was on full alert too. A Box handler had been called out to meet a source in Antrim. The source was ex PIRA and said he had vital information regarding something coming in from the mainland. Everyone held their breath, only to find it was a drug deal. Normally an excellent result, but not in this case.

At the Liverpool boat, Desmond booked his BMW on for the afternoon sailing to Dublin. There were no problems encountered and he had ensured that the aluminium case was safely stored in the boot. He had secured the case with an elastic strap fitted to his car. This should guarantee that his cargo would arrive safely, all intact and ready to go. He collected his papers and wallet from the car and walked to the stairs. In the boot the liquids were motionless, separated by the stainless steel of the container. None of the fellow travellers knew how close they were to the deadly cargo as they squeezed past the locked BMW and made their way to the stairwell.

CHAPTER 14

Things were tense in the Dale too. Not only the sarin gas escapade and the endless waiting to be tasked at a moments notice but there was a tension between Marc and Jenny. After her briefing Jenny had asked to be taken into Ballyclare as she needed to get some things. Marc pulled the black BMW coupe out of the garage and was waiting in the drive as she left the house. He jumped from the drivers seat and opened the passenger door for her. She paused just before she got into the car and looked at Marc.

'Why thank you sir', she said.

Jenny was still in her jeans and sweater. Marc parked in the square in the town centre and locked the car after she exited. The alarm chirped twice and the direction indicator lights flashed briefly. They walked around the town and window shopped mostly. In the chemist Jenny bought shampoo and makeup before returning to Marc at the doorway. She linked her arm through his and leaned into him, brushing his ear with a kiss. Marc flushed red again. She suggested coffee and buns, her treat, and he agreed. The two found a small, cosy cafe and settled down at a window table. With a cappuccino each on the table top, the pair sat in silence for a few minutes then Jenny spoke.

'Marc, last night, in my room. You, well you said . . . you loved me?

'I wasn't . . . I mean I didn't . . . Oh . . . 'stammered Marc

'It's OK, if you feel that way. I feel something too'.

'You do?', Marc asked.

'There are feelings I have that you have awakened. I have not felt this way in a very long time'.

Marc blushed and looked down at his coffee. Jenny smiled and reached over touching his hand. Their eyes met and once again Marc was all but lost. Jenny squeezed his hand and added;

'Let's take it slowly, eh?'

Marc nodded. They leaned forward and kissed gently. Jenny followed it with a smile. The whole cafe seemed to lighten up and Marc found himself again caught in her beaming grin. He smiled too. It felt good. Really good. He squeezed her hand and both began to laugh. A short while later Jenny despatched Marc to get the car as she said she had one last shop to visit. She watched him walk toward the Square to retrieve the BMW and she dashed across into the jewellers. Several minutes later she emerged and joined Marc at the vehicle.

Marc fired up the six cylinder engine and the BMW purred away towards home. Well, home for now at least. Stopping in the driveway of the house Marc noticed that Jay's car was gone. Gym, he thought. Jay will train until he is ninety Marc laughed to himself. For the first time in a very long time he felt comfortable in his own skin. He knew Jenny was the reason; something had started. She was so easy to be with, her charm and beauty had overwhelmed him. His heart had been stolen. Well and truly stolen and he had been an eager participant in it's theft. As the car rolled to a halt Jenny leaned across him and slipped a small box into his hand. Marc was surprised.

'Is this for me?' he asked sheepishly.

'Indeed'. She beamed.

Opening it he found a silver bracelet, hand hammered with a metal folded knot in the centre. It was a rigid bracelet, quite wide but very thin.

'Wow, thank you'. Stammered Marc, 'It's beautiful'.

Jenny beamed again. Her smile was sunshine. They kissed. On the way into the house Marc slipped the bracelet on. In his profession operatives were discouraged from wearing anything that may identify them or may stand out or be different. He wore a silver TAG watch with a plain white face on his left wrist and now had an adornment for his right. He loved the bracelet, he could slide it under his shirt cuff when he needed to hide it and display it the rest of the time.

'I'm glad you like it', Jenny said.

'I do. I really do. You are very thoughtful and full of surprises'.

'You think?'

'I think'.

Finding the house empty Jenny turned to Marc and said;

'My room for a proper de brief?'

Marc nodded and the two scampered upstairs giggling like teenagers.

Sixty miles away the abbot pulled into the services just before Dungannon on the M1 motorway. He switched the engine off and reached for his mobile phone. Scrolling down he stopped at the Brigadier's number. His bigger than average finger dialled the number and he put the old phone to his ear. It was ringing.

'Hello'

'Hi brig, it's abbot'.

'Oh, bout ye big man?'

'Aye OK. Listen did you find anything out about Mickey Doyle yet?'

'You not heard Abbot. Mickey got nutted this mornin. Reckon it the Chinks. Remember wee Barry said they were all put out about the cannabis deal?'

'Nutted?' exclaimed the Abbot

'Oh aye. Head job. One shot. He was in his office in the pub in Antrim. Aye he is tatie bread like. No mistake'.

'Fuking hell Brig'.

'Are you paid abbot like. Did he owe you any money?'.

'I'm half paid but it's all I want to be. I'm in deeper than I figured on this one Brig'.

'You need anything Abbot?'.

'Aye. My wee envelope I left with you and the blue holdall. Can you drop them in the flat in the Coole for me?.

'Ok I will leave the envelope in the normal place and put the bag in the bunker?'

'Cheers brig. There is some cash in the envelope, take what you need for doing this and thanks mate'.

Aw fuck me abbot, no way. No way, you're a mate and I owe you I think. This ones on me. Take it you will have to scarper for a while?.

'I intend to. Gotta go. Thanks Brig, cheers'.

'Aye take her easy big man. See ya'.

The Abbot sat in silence for a few minutes, then lifted the mobile again and dialled a number from memory. This time the phone rang very briefly;

'43131', said an English voice.

'It's two one nine. I need to speak with someone', said The Abbot.

'Just a second'.

The Abbot waited and gazed out his windscreen. What a clusterfuck, he thought. At least he had half the money paid up front. That was always a good idea. Poor Mickey, bet he did not see that coming.

'Is that two one nine?' asked another very polite English voice.

'Yes'.

'I need to verify. Can you give me the first four figures of your date of birth please?'

'Yes. Two zero eleven'.

'And the last handler number?'

'eight one five seven'.

'and finally your codename?'

'Kestrel'.

'How can I help you Mr Donovan?' asked the silky smooth voice.

'I have an item in my possession that I think you may be very interested in. A black plastic flask. From Porton I believe?'

There was a few seconds silence the silky voice said;

'Can you contact me by landline?'

'Negative. No can do. Are you interested?'.

'Yes we are very interested. Where are you?'

'Stay on this number and I shall ring you later and we can sort an exchange'.

The Abbot rang off. Getting out of his car he walked a short distance to the nearest metal storm drain and dropped the mobile into it. Then without a backward glance he climbed into the Saab and started the engine. Pulling the automatic gear selector into drive he shoulder checked and drove off. Pulling onto the M1 motorway he accelerated away. He knew they would be locating his call and trying to activate the mobile at this very minute. Good luck he thought. Only the sewer rats would be able to speak with them now.

At PSNI Headquarters at Knock in Belfast the Emergency planning Department were getting busy. Four of the front line TSG units were on twentyfour hour stand-by. NBC kits and respirators complete with canisters and radioactive particle detectors were being tested and re-tested. The red telephone in the commanders 'Com-Sec' office began to ring and an already overstretched Chief Inspector lifted the hand set.

At number ten Downing Street another red telephone was ringing too. The Home Secretary's, already overstretched, P.A. reached for the handset.

Back at the Dale, Marc's blackberry began to ring. An arm, wearing a silver bracelet, reached out from under the duvet cover and picked up the mobile.

'Hello'.

'Mr Marc?'

'Speaking'.

'It's Mr Edward. We have a situation. Stand by to be patched through to Mr Wilner'.

Marc listened intently to his instructions. He terminated his call and immediately rang Jay. His instructions to Jay were clear, return to the Dale ASAP. As Marc was finishing his call Jenny was already in the shower. It looked like they were on. At last. Action.

CHAPTER 15

The Abbot pulled off the M1 motorway and into Sprucefield retail park. Leaving the Saab he walked briskly to the Networld mobile telephone shop. Here he purchased two pay-as-you-go handsets, two different network sim cards and an in car charger He paid in cash and produced his false drivers licence as identification. Back at the Saab he unwrapped the in car charger and plugged it into the cigar lighter. As he drove back towards Belfast the first handset was connected up, he could see the small battery symbol displayed flashing as it took a full current. Both phones remained switched off. He had also bought a Collins roadmap. The Saab had needed fuel and he decided to stop at a petrol station to fill up. Here he bought sandwiches and bottled water. As he munched his way through the food he studied his map. A short time later he unplugged his mobile and swapped the charger to the second phone. For this journey it would charge enough to complete his task.

The Abbot drove off towards Lisburn and after several miles stopped at The Cutts public house. He frequented here from time to time and was familiar with the pub's lay out. In the entrance hall he located an alcove with a payphone in it. Pulling out some paper from his wallet he dialled the same number as before. The phone answered almost immediately. The Abbot drew himself closer to the alcove and began to speak.

'This is Kestrel'.

'Yes Mr Donovan', said a silky smooth English voice, 'We were about to discuss the handover?'

'Aye, first I need two hundred and fifty thousand pounds. Paid into my Zurich account or no deal'.

'That's not a problem'.

'In sterling?'

'But of course. Have you an account number?'

The Abbot read out the account numbers and letters and the name and password required to lodge money electronically. There was silence for a few seconds and then silky voice read the same information back to him. Abbot noticed the perfect training. Silky voice was echoing his request. Checking and double checking.

'The money will be paid when we have the item', said silky voice.

'I don't think so, it will be paid now or no deal'.

'Ok, it will be in your account shortly'.

'I will check it and ring you back'.

The Abbot disconnected and hung up the phone. There was no point in ringing to check. They agreed to pay a vast sum with no hesitation, no barter or proof he even had the item. Abbot knew he was a dead man to them. Dead and buried. Even now he could see his file on their desk, his photos and details being given to some other Abbot. Some other killer, hitman, stiffer, whatever they chose to call him. He knew he was dead. He made a last minute check of the hallway just in case they had installed a security camera in the pub, but it was the same as always. He knew in several minutes an operative would be lifting this very hand set and talking to silky voice. He wiped the receiver with a coat sleeve, then walked briskly to the Saab.

Mr Wilner's phone rang at the CTO's main office at Vauxhall in London.

'Hello, Mr Wilner here'.

'Ah, Mister Wilner. Glad I caught you old boy. It's Jerome Fielding-Hall here from Military Int HQ at Chicksands down in sunny Bedfordshire'.

'Yes Mr Fielding-Hall, what can I do for you?'

'Oh please call me Jerome. My people have been in contact with an old asset we used to have in Ulster. I believe you have some people there might help me?'

'How can we help you?'

'Well you see old chap this asset has an item of ours from Porton Down. Ring any bells?'

'Yes I am aware of the item'.

'Well it seems he will sell it back to us. We need some of your chaps to collect it. I'm told you have a boffin of some sort there?'

'Boffin?' Wilner almost laughed out aloud.

'Yes one of those science chappies'.

'We do indeed'.

'Good, only I need it collected and verified PDQ if you get my meaning?'

'Yes I understand. What about the asset?'

'Oh we will look after him as he was one of ours and all that jazz'.

'What information have you at present?'

'I have a chap heading round to give your people all the gen and what have you. Just putting you in the loop so to speak. Well good chatting, must go chin chin'.

Wilner replaced his phone. He knew Jerome Fielding-Hall of old. He was just plain old Jerome Fielding in those days. Wilner had served in Ulster in the seventies and eighties and his military unit had briefly encountered the Force Research Unit or FRU as they called themselves. Jerome Fielding was a Captain in the FRU then. They were an undercover unit with questionable methods. Although they got results against the PIRA their working practices were very similar, capturing terrorist suspects, alleged torture, executions, double crosses and all the vile, murky, undercover, underworld subterfuge that shares that genre. The military denied their existence. The Prime Minister requested their disbandment. Although they were stood down in the main, their operations still ran from time to time. Wilner felt a cold shiver along his spine. This was just what he needed. A FRU type operation with an 'old asset from Ulster' at it's centre. He lifted his phone and dialled a number.

The Brigadier pulled up outside the Abbot's flat in Rathcoole. As promised he opened the front door and walked into the musty hallway. Gathering up the mail he set it on the hall table. It was an old, rickety half moon table. Dark walnut with a small, fine gold edging. It, like the rest of the flat, had seen better days. Closing the door the Brigadier opened the small drawer in the front of table. Reaching into his inside coat pocket he removed the Abbot's envelope and dropped it into the drawer. Closing it gently in case the drawer should break.

Walking through the small kitchen the Brigadier opened the back door and stepped out into the enclosed yard. Here he opened the lid of the plastic coal bunker and deposited the blue holdall and the weapon it contained.

The Burner as the abbot called it. It was a Franchi SPAS combat shotgun with it were several cartridges in a card board box. The holdall gently came to rest on the half full coal bunker. The Brigadier closed the lid, re-entered the house, retracing his steps to the front door. He cautiously opened the door and walked back to his car. Job done, as they say.

Two hours later the Abbot stood beside the small pool of water in the old Blue Circle cement works limestone quarry at Magheramorne near Larne. He knew this area well as he had used it over the years for all sorts of tasks, training, torture, beatings and the occasional murder had all been carried out here. He was very familiar with the layout of the quarry and always liked to fight on his home ground. The Saab was parked beside an old limestone outbuilding with no roof which had been a pump house thirty years ago. The quarry was disused these many years, having been reduced from a main cement production plant to a grinding facility. Then a store area for old, unused machinery and eventually closed for good. There was a security man on the main gate but the Abbot knew eight or ten different exits, some accessible by car and some only accessible by foot, well away from the main buildings and prying eyes.

The Abbot was staring at the carcass of an old crane. It's rusty cab had been yellow at one point but was now red. Red with rust. Grass and weeds grew from the drivers seat and a birds nest was visible half way along its erect jib. It looked like a prehistoric relic from another time. A once graceful creature reduced now to a rotting hulk. One track was missing, the other was completely rusted. The links were solid. This crane would never drive again.

It's jib would never lift any heavy articles or pull a drag bucket. Walking forward the Abbot placed the flask onto the only solid piece of bodywork he could find, just beside the drivers door. He took out his phone and dialled the number. He spoke briefly then set the phone up beside the flask.

Turning quickly he drove the Saab out of the quarry and parked on the Ballylig Road, a small side road under the cover of some trees. He quickly attached his pistols to his body in the normal way and returned to the crane wreck on foot. He knew that they would locate the mobile signal and come to get the flask. He thought they would come by helicopter. He thought they would bring a team to take him down. He picked his spot, away from the crane, in the dense undergrowth. Wriggling into position he settled down to wait.

In the CTO office in Vauxhall, Christian Blake's computer screen illuminated. It was showing the number the Military Intelligence guys had given him for the Abbot. Christian hammered in some numbers and letters and the mobile phone became live. He saw the Abbot had disconnected the call and turned the phone off but Christian had located it and would now follow it's every movement.

CHAPTER 16

Marc, Jay and Jenny were on board the Nissan Xtrail. Jay was driving and Marc was on the Blackberry;

'Mr Marc, it's Mr Christian. We have an activation on a mobile telephone which is static at Magheramorne quarry near Larne. Do you know where that is or do you need co-ordinates?',

'No I know the quarry. Who is the target?'.

'A Sean Donovan. He is ex-military and has worked with our colleagues in military intelligence in Ulster. He is a native of Northern Ireland and a category one in the danger stakes. Understood?'.

'Yes. Keep me posted on any movement on the mobile or any other changes'.

'Will do. Remember we just want the item. Get it anyway that you can. I think Military intelligence are going to take care of Mr Donovan'.

The phones disconnected. Marc realised that a category one was a very dangerous operative. There were three categories listed. Category three was normally a sleeper or source with no history of violence and low in the security stakes. Category two on the other hand had some knowledge of operations, normally an operative or specialist. They required more attention to detail in the day to day dealings, hard to trace, hard to catch and harder to take down. A category one, well, that was an operative or asset who had attained rogue status. Normally a shoot on sight for operatives like Mark and Jay and a 'T-OP' or target of opportunity for the sniper types.He glanced at Jay, who had heard the conversation on the Blackberry's loudspeaker. Both men knew that Military intelligence would only have given CTO the bare bones of the information they shared. They would have to be very vigilant and at least one step ahead on this one.

At RAF Aldergrove a black Bell Jet Ranger helicopter started it's engine. A small plume of blue exhaust gas came from the top port and the lazy blades began to spin. From the military hangar a tall thin man emerged carrying a long nylon bag. He walked briskly to the chopper and climbed into the front seat. Donning headphones he spoke very briefly with the pilot. The bell had been despatched several hours before from a naval base at Faslane in Scotland. It had been waiting here on the tarmac for the final instructions. The tall man unrolled a military map and his long, bony index finger pointed to the quarry and the outlying areas. Brief discussion over, decision made, the chopper lifted her tail briefly before the main body wobbled it's way skyward. At forty feet above ground the pilot turned through a full three hundred and sixty degrees. Tall man smiled to himself, even on a runway these special forces pilots carry out their training and checks. A few seconds later they were off. Flying low and fast across the fertile Ulster countryside.

Marc and Jay were making their way across country too. Deciding to take the country roads and approach the quarry through the main gate. Marc reached into the rear seat and lifted out the small black nylon bag that sat beside Jenny. He pulled the bag into the passengers footwell between his legs.

'Anything we should know about this gas Jenny?'. He asked one last time.

'No. Just show me the canister and I will deal with it. If it is punctured or leaking get as far away as possible. Remember wear the respirators that I have given you until I am able to place the canister in the sealed containers.'.

There were three plastic containers in the trunk of the Nissan. They fitted one inside the other, like Russian dolls. Jenny would isolate the canister in these containers until she could test the two liquids and confirm it was Sarin components.

The Bell helicopter skirted around the quarry rim before dropping into a large agricultural field close to the perimeter fence. The tall man ran from the chopper, crouched forward and carrying the long black bag. When he was clear he turned and gave the thumbs up sign to the pilot. Again he watched a complete three sixty turn and seconds later the chopper was gone.

The Abbot heard the chopper. Faintly at first, becoming louder and louder. Ordinary people may not have heard it or have dismissed it as background noise. Ambient noise, picked up and processed by the sub conscious brain but never alerted within the conscious mind. But the Abbot, well, he had lain in wait for choppers many times. His ears strained and would pick out the definite chopping sound as the broad blades beat through the air. Then the deeper whap whap noise as the blades change pitch just before touch down. The Abbot could not see it, but he knew it was there and he could feel it's deadly cargo all around. His common sense told him he should leave, but there was an overwhelming sense of duty telling him to stay. Although a killer without mercy, the Abbot could not walk away from a Sarin gas canister. He had to know it had been given into safe hands and more importantly he had to see who they had sent to kill him. Reaching into his jacket pocket he rubbed the wooden butt of the Mauser and breathed deeply. Soon, he thought, soon this would be over.

The tall man felt his way along the chain link fence. He had spotted several large gaps in the fence as the chopper circled before landing. He too had spent many years waiting on, flying in and shooting from these unlikely birds. Finding a gap big enough to squeeze through he made his way to the undergrowth. From his pocket he produced a mobile phone. Fitting an earpiece he dialled a number. A brief conversation ensued and the tall man was guided to a lower ledge on the old quarry face. From here his caller said he should be within six hundred metres of the transmitting phone. He opened his long nylon bag and drew out the rifle.

The Abbot moved around gingerly inside his tree and bushes hide. Scanning the ridges high on the quarry he looked for movement or a reflection or fleeting shadow. Nothing. He watched, holding his breath he listened. All he could hear was his heartbeat. Opening his mouth slightly removed the heart beat noise. In the very far distance, faintly, he heard the noise of a diesel engine.

In the Nissan Marc was talking on the Blackberry. He was being told that the mobile signal was in the centre of the quarry floor and close to a disused pump house. The Garmin sat-nav was displaying a red X on the spot where the signal was coming from. This was no ordinary sat-nav but one that the Technical department at CTO had modified. It was receiving signals from the static phone via the CTO base at Chelmsford.

The tall man scanned the area with his digital monocular. He swept the pump house and the small lake, he saw nothing of interest. As he swept the crane wreck he noticed something beside the cab. Focussing deliberately on it he saw it was a black flask. He was, however, unable to see the small mobile telephone pushed into the driving track of the rusting crane just a few inches from the flask. 'Bingo', he muttered. The monocular told the distance to the flask was five hundred and sixty four metres. Now the tall man lay prone along the path. He began to crawl forward to the edge of the rim, pushing his rifle in front of him, looking for a perfect firing position. He could feel the cold, damp Ulster ground underneath him. It permeated into his core. He flipped the spring loaded bipod out from the front of the rifle and removed his sight covers. Then a slow, deliberate leopard crawl and a turning of his body to suit the shot angle. Elbows control the direction of the weapon, left to right and knees control the height of the weapon. Soon the rifle was drawn down on it's target. Waiting to spit death with a 7.62 fully jacketed round nestling in the chamber. A new one hundred and seventy grain Lapau made round.

Tall man carried an AI AW sniper rifle. Made by Accuracy International it was black, had a spring loaded Harris type bi-pod on the front and came with the choice of a five round or eight round magazine. He had an eight round magazine fitted but had only five rounds loaded. Tall man also carried a standard Glock nineteen nine millimetre pistol in a belt holster. He had removed it and stored it in the rifle's long nylon bag as it hurt him when he

95

was in the prone position. His chosen sight was a Schmidt and Bender PM 2. It was plain and simple, not unlike tall man himself and had standard cross hairs. It was a three to twelve times fifty magnification sight. It made the flask seem so close that he could almost grab it. He had shot with the other sights, new digital sights with laser and thermal fittings and all the plethora of the high-tech generation. He liked simple. It normally worked. This sight was just that. A sight, manufactured to the highest quality. Easy to use, uncomplicated and not reliant on anything except the operator. Tall man pushed his eye to the sight reaching the point of full bloom and smiled.

At the main gate Marc showed his security services pass to a somewhat startled security guard. The fat guard had seen several film crews here over the past few years but never the secret service. As they pulled away into the quarry proper Marc opened the black bag at his feet. He passed a respirator to Jenny and then to Jay. He held the mask in his hand and looked at it. It looked like a black monster face staring back at him. Massive eyes and a canister on the mouth piece, it looked like a monster's death grimace. He again reached into the bag and drew out a Heckler and Koch MP5 machine pistol. Snapping on a thirty round magazine, he pushed the stock release catch at the rear and drew out the small, retractable stock. Finally he cocked the weapon. The sudden snap as the working parts came forward made Jenny jump.

The approaching noise of the Nissan made the Abbot draw out his Mauser pistol. His big thumb flicked off the safety, just in case.

High above, on the ledge, the tall man heard the approaching engine too. He dialled the preset number and spoke on answer.

'Standby, vehicle approaching'.

'Alright', said silky voice.

Jay stopped the Nissan short of the target area. Marc whispered to Jenny that they would check the area and then send for her. She pulled a face but Marc could see she was frightened. He gave in and agreed that she should stay with him. After all, Jenny was no operative but a scientist and this was definitely not in her job description. She was extremely keen to find the gas, however, as she understood better that most the ramifications of it remaining at large.

Marc and Jay fanned out after fitting respirators. Jay going to the right of the old pump house, walking on the balls of his feet. His Glock pistol in an extended grip in both hands held out to his front. Marc went to the left of the house with Jenny close behind. He noticed the metal shutter, which had at one time covered the rear window of the pump house was now missing at one corner. The metal screen hung loose, like a book leaf and exposed an area where the pump house interior could be observed. Marc crept forward and tried to see inside the building. It was impossible to see properly inside the clumsy rubber headgear.He had the MP5 pulled well into his shoulder. Both men were still not visible to the Abbot or the tall man.

Jenny on the other hand, wandered away from Marc slightly to his left. She was looking at the crane jib that she could partially see behind the pump house. She found herself moving forward and all at once the old crane wreck came into view. There, sitting proud, was a black plastic flask. Jenny could hardly believe her luck. Without thinking she tightened her respirator and dashed toward the crane.

'I have one person approaching target', said tall man.

'Is it Kestrel?', enquired silky voice.

'Cannot confirm. Respirator on'.

'Is it Kestrel?'

'I say again I cannot confirm. I don't think so'.

'How close to target?'

'Ten metres. Am still unable to confirm. Five metres'.

'If it touches target take it out'.

'At target now'.

'Touching it?'

'Rodger'.

'Take the shot'.

'Confirm your last'.

I say again shoot shoot shoot'.

The tall man's bony finger took first pressure on the trigger. Breath in, out, hold, relax, his brain told him. Somewhere in that thought cycle between hold and relax he squeezed the trigger.

The Abbot was scanning the ridge when he saw the muzzle flash. Gottcha, he said to himself and he reversed out of his hiding place. He began to run towards the road hoping to find the shooter before he left his position.

Marc could see no one inside the pump house and turned in time to see Jenny run off. He called to her but his voice was lost inside the respirator. As he rounded the corner of the pump house he saw her tall, slender figure at the crane. A split second later he saw her head explode inside her rubber mask. A high velocity shot rang out and Marc's training kicked in. He fired a three shot burst from the MP5 directing it at the quarry ridge. He hoped this would disorient the sniper and allow him time to trail Jenny from the kill zone.

At the same time Jay saw the Abbot break cover. The Abbot turned when he heard the MP5's burst. For a split second Jay and him locked eyes before opening fire on each other as they dived for cover. Jay had managed four rounds to the Abbot's three. The Glock and the Mauser, separated by more than thirty years of design, were doing their thing as the Americans say. The Abbot had missed his target although he had clipped the canister on Jay's respirator. Jay too had missed, but only just. The Abbot heard the whizz of two rounds go past his head. What he didn't know was one was to his left the other his right and they missed by centimetres. Jay trailed off his respirator, gas or no he thought I need to be able to see my target. The Abbot was gone into the dense undergrowth like a gazelle with Jay in hot pursuit.

The tall man withdrew from the ridge and spoke quickly on the phone. The plan had been for him to kill the asset then collect the canister before being extracted by chopper.

'Target eliminated. Cannot get to canister area now unfriendly'.

'Get the canister'. Said silky voice, starting to sound flustered.

'Negative, not at this time'.

'Get the fucking canister as instructed that's an order'.

'No can do, it's Dodge city down there. Multiple targets'.

'Can chopper land and retrieve?'.

'Negative, negative. LZ too hot for dustoff. Task him as I need exfil'.

'Negative. I am ordering you to go on foot and retrieve'.

The tall man pulled his earpiece out and packed away his rifle. Drawing his Glock he began to jog back to the drop off point. Fucking spooks he thought. Get his own canister.

Marc reached Jenny. Her slender body lay on her side as if asleep. The respirator was still on her head. Gently removing it Marc found the entry wound just at her right temple. Dropping to his knees he cradled her head and cried. Probably for the first time ever in his life. The emotion overwhelmed him. His shock and sadness gave way to anger. Sniper, right, lets kill him right now. Scanning along the rim of the quarry he saw nothing. He couldn't leave Jenny here so he picked her up in his arms. He carried her to the Nissan. Her long auburn hair was matted with blood. She was still warm, he could feel her body heat as he carried her. Her left arm hung away from her body in an arc. Lifeless. Dead. The MP5 slung around Marc also swung from side to side. Like a pendulum, it too seemed lifeless. His hopes, dreams, aspirations, all gone in an instant. Gone at the pull of a trigger, the bark of a gun, the request of some spook. At the Nissan Marc placed her on the ground. Propping her up against the rear wheel. Now for the first time he saw the exit wound. It was just as he expected. Horrific. Massive. Ugly. Poor Jenny.

The abbot was running uphill making for the main road, ducking and diving between tree branches and old rusted machinery parts. He halted every now and again and fired off a round to keep Jay at a distance. The Abbot's exit point to the main road and the tall man's were the same place. Tall man stopped, noticing the movement to his right on the lower ground. He pressed himself flat into the quarry face into a small crag. Seconds later the Abbot hurtled into view in full flight, he crashed through the brush and scrub before jumping through the hole in the fence and disappearing into the dense undergrowth. Two shots rang out, making the tall man flinch. They were close, very close. Jay appeared again just below him on the ridge. He was aiming at the gap in the fence and the fleeing Abbot. Two more shots and then Jay jumped through the fence too and was lost in the undergrowth.

The tall man blew out a long breath. That was close. Both men were so determined to make the gap in the fence that they literally passed the tall man's position by a few yards and never noticed him. He squeezed out of the crack in the rock face and ran down the path. I'm not following them he thought. Best option is into the bowels of the quarry and call for the chopper. Imagine his surprise when he rounded the corner and saw the canister still sitting on the crane. Jackpot, he thought, and jogged over to it.

The downhill bank was very steep and extremely slippery as the Abbot careered down it at full speed. There were dense trees and shrubs on both sides, however, he could just make out the road below. His Saab was less than a mile away and he would be glad to see it. All of a sudden two hammer blows struck his back. Something punched the left hand side of his neck and sent him spinning. As he fell into the undergrowth he heard the shots. Lots of shots. His right hand lost grip on the Mauser and it dropped into the undergrowth. The Abbot was shot and no mistake.

Jay stood on the bank the smoking Glock still in his two handed grip. The gun was roasting hot and the metal was making a ticking noise as it cooled in the county Antrim chill. The polymer slide was locked to the rear and the barrel protruded alone, smoking slightly. He had managed to get a clear sight of the target, both hands up into the aim and he emptied the pistol at the fleeing man. He was unsure the exact number of rounds he fired, he guessed at least ten. He knew that he had hit the Abbot on his back. As he started down the bank to find the body, Jay's left thumb pressed the magazine release catch on his Glock. Drawing the magazine out he dropped it into his pocket and drew out a fully loaded one, from his belt pouch pushing it home. His right thumb was about to press down on the slide when he saw it. Him. The Abbot. Standing only a few yards away, in the undergrowth. It was definitely him, but how?. As the Glock slide snapped forward on Jay's pistol the Abbot fired. He was holding a Mauser in his left hand and he fired four shots in quick succession. Jay collapsed into the undergrowth discharging an un-aimed shot. The Abbot had lost one pistol and was not intending to look for it. He was bleeding badly from a flesh wound to his neck and was cut and bruised from his fall. He stumbled onto the road and began to jog toward the Saab.

The tall man approached the crane slowly. He could see no body although there was lots of blood. It must have been removed he thought. Head shot. No way it's still alive. He set the long black nylon bag up against the crane and lifted the flask. He replaced his earpiece and redialled.

'What's going on?' asked silky voice.

'I have it. Send exfil to quarry floor'.

'Confirm you have it. The canister'.

'I have it, intact, not damaged. Now send the chopper'.

The phone rang off. The tall man turned and found himself looking down the business end of an MP5 and a very angry Marc.

'Set the canister down', spat Marc. The tall man complied, extending his right arm and leaving the canister back on the track. All the time his eyes never left Marc's. Marc looked down at the long black nylon bag, and so did the tall man. His gaze returned back to the tall man's face. Their eyes met again and Marc felt his finger's tighten on the trigger.

'You fucking piece of shit, you killed my . . . I mean the science officer'.

Tall man sensed something else here. My science officer he thought. That's odd.

'Who are you', asked Marc.

'Mil-Int. I work for 44 Ops.

'Sniper?, said Marc nodding at the bag.

'Yes sniper'.

'You got any other guns?'

'Yeah, Glock'.

'Pull it'.

'Go to hell. If your going to shoot me get on with it'.

Marc was surprised at his frankness. Right he thought. I am.

A sudden yell made Marc look over his shoulder. Jay was staggering down the quarry, he was covered in blood. Several yard away he collapsed. Marc ran toward him leaving the tall man and the gas to themselves. The tall man exhaled for the second time that day.

Jay was bleeding from the chest and abdomen. Marc pulled his Blackberry and dialled.

'Two officers down. One dead one seriously injured. Request immediate extraction and medevac from this location'. Then turning to the tall man he snapped,' At the Nissan, in the boot, big first aid bag bring it, now'.

The tall man turned and ran off. Marc busied himself with Jay. He was a mess and no mistake. There was a sucking chest wound, it was obvious that his lung had collapsed. How did you manage to walk this far thought Marc. The tall man appeared with the giant Bergen and knelt to help Marc.

'You got cling film?' he asked

'Yeah in the Bergen'.

'You wrap his chest and I will get the IV set up with the fluids, ok?'

Marc nodded. Both men worked with professional ease. Marc noticed that the tall man was calm and very confident. The whup whup of an approaching helicopter made both men look up. It was the tall man's ride. He glanced at Marc;

'Tell them to have a team at Antrim area Hospital on stand by. We will take my chopper. Ok?' Said the tall man.

Marc dialled on the Blackberry and relayed the information. Marc helped Jay into the rear of the chopper. He was almost blue in colour and his eyes were glazing over. The tall man climbed in the front after collecting the gas and the long black nylon bag.

'Antrim area hospital', said the tall man.

'No can do, boss wants the package soon as, sorry'.

The tall man produced his Glock and aimed it at the pilots head.

'I can fly this. So don't fuck with me. Hospital now'.

The Bell took off skyward and set a course for the hospital. Marc was in shock. Holding Jay's arm in his hand to keep it steady he held the plasma bag in the other. The tall man was on the phone;

'Look you fuck', he spat, 'I have just killed a science officer at your request. Now get a clean up team to the quarry pronto. There is a jeep and a body to recover. You will get your package when I have delivered mine'.

He turned to Marc, 'You CTO?'.

Marc nodded.

At the heli-pad at Antrim Hospital an ambulance and two doctors placed Jay on a trolley before lifting it into the ambulance. They worked for several minutes with him before driving off to the accident and emergency department. Marc realised that he had to accompany Jay until more help arrived. The tall man climbed back into the chopper and Marc approached him ;

'My MP5 is in the rear of the Bell. Can you see that it's delivered to CTO?'

The tall man nodded. With that the chopper climbed skyward.

CHAPTER 17

The Saab rolled steadily along the main roads through Carrickfergus and onto Rathcoole. The Abbot held his left hand up to his neck trying to curtail the bleeding from the flesh wound. It stung. It really, really stung. Parking three streets away he made his way to the flat trying to remain unseen. It would have been difficult as he looked a sight, covered in mud and debris from the quarry. Soaking wet and bleeding badly from a neck wound. No one stopped him or asked any questions. Rathcoole was that sort of place. Mind your own, was the motto here. He made his way along the rear entry, approaching his flat from the back door, the kitchen door. Opening the rear gate he lifted the lid on the coalbunker and removed the blue bag it contained.

Inside he locked the door and set the bag up on the old formica topped table. The Mauser quickly followed. Then he gently slipped off his jacket, letting it fall to the floor. The Abbot pulled off his pullover with his left hand as his right hand was all but useless. There he stood, wearing his old white, Kevlar body armour. Undoing the Velcro straps he swung the two parts onto the table. There below the makers name, 'second-chance', were the heads of three nine millimetre rounds. Two were side by side, maybe two inches apart. The third was well beneath them and was the reason that his right kidney was so sore. He grinned. Nice shooting he thought. Second chance indeed.

The Abbot opened the cupboard and lifted out a bottle of Bushmills malt. Pouring a generous glass he rummaged in the cupboard and found some paracetamol. Popping two tablets he took a gulp. The hot liquid burned the back of his throat and took his breath away. He watched the alcohol cling to the sides of the glass. Staggering to the bathroom he filled the wash basin and extracted an old first aid kit from the spare bedroom. Lots of savlon and gauze squares later he was sporting a neat dressing to the left side of his neck. An examination in the bathroom mirror revealed two bruises on his back, deeper and heavier than all the others. He had a feeling that his right shoulder blade may be fractured but a hospital visit was out of the question. All in all the soft Kevlar had stopped the rounds penetrating. Had he not been wearing it, well, that would be a very different tale.

The Abbot washed quickly and dumped his old dirty clothes in a heap on the bedroom floor. Fresh jeans and trainers and a dry sweatshirt and he was a new man. Opening the cupboard underneath the sink in the kitchen he quickly removed a loose board. Feeling inside he drew out a small, hessian bag. The clink of fresh nine millimetre rounds made him smile. He had lost one of his babies, his old familiar, old faithful Mauser. However, he still had it's twin. Time to reload.

The VW Passat parked in the car park at Antrim area hospital. Mr Thomas had been ringing Marc's Blackberry but to no avail. He locked the car and walked briskly to the doors of A&E. Accident and Emergency, he thought, passing the red and white sign. It should say clusterfuck instead. The corridor was bathed in an ultra bright white light and had the smell of disinfectant mixed with vomit and other bodily fluids. At the reception window he produced a police identification pass and told the lady he was CID and needed to speak with the man who accompanied the gunshot victim. She directed him to the correct area. He pocketed the false identity pass and was on his way. Security service passes were way too complicated to explain to receptionists and aroused too many interests.

Marc looked up as he heard the approaching footsteps.

'Mr Marc?', enquired the voice.

Marc nodded.

'I'm Mr Thomas'. The strong Glaswegian accent and the short hair cut filled in the rest of the gaps. Another CTO operative. No doubt about it.

'How is Mr. Jay?'

'He's still in theatre. Must be there an hour or so'.

Thomas stared at Marc when he stood up. He was covered in blood and soaking wet. His hands were black. He looked like death warmed up.

'Bloody hell man. You better get back to the Dale and get cleaned up. I'm here to watch Jay'.

'Yeah, thanks mate', stuttered Marc.

'Here are keys to a Passat. Top car park. It's silver. OK?'

'Yeah, OK'.

'I'll call you when I know more'.

Marc nodded and Thomas smiled. Mr Thomas had been an SAS operative at the same time as Jay. They were well acquainted. He felt Marc's pain although men such as these go a long way to disguise hurt and anguish.

The cold air outside the hospital hit Marc like the opening of a freezer door. He shivered but felt strangely detached. His Blackberry began to vibrate. Retrieving it from his pocket he noticed several missed calls. There had been no signal reception in the waiting area outside the operating theatre.

Answering the phone he found himself talking to Mr Christian.

'Mr Marc, Mr Christian. Are you alright?'.

'Yeah. I'll live'.

'Any update on Mr Jay?'

'No. Still in theatre'.

'Mr Wilner wants a sit-rep re the shooting of the science officer. Porton are going ape'.

'Sniper. One of the military intelligence boys. Tall thin fellow. Was it a blue on blue?'

'Yes it would appear so'.

'Who gave the fire order?'

'Don't know. Mr Wilner will fill in the blanks on that one'.

'They have the canister. I'm going back to the Dale. Where is the science officer now?'

'A clean up team has brought her back to RAF Aldergrove. They have the Nissan too and some weapons. I will call you when I know more'.

'Thats OK'.

'Why was the science officer on her own?'

'She wasn't. Jenny was behind me, I stopped to clear an outbuilding, she must have seen the canister and went for it. I only knew she was gone when I heard the shot'.

'I will pass that on. Call you later'.

The phone went dead and Marc's feelings went dead too. Numb. Empty.

109

Arriving at the Dale he found the Nissan parked in the driveway. Marc noticed that it had recently been washed. The driveway was dry in the main, but he noticed the small line of water that had run off the bodywork when the jeep had been parked. Inside the house he found his MP5 and Jay's Glock on the table in the kitchen. There were car keys and Jay's mobile telephone. The clean up team certainly had done just that.

Walking upstairs he gingerly pushed Jenny's bedroom door open. The room was bare. Bed made. All regular, but no trace that Jenny had ever been there at all. Marc felt his emotions well up again. He made an effort to undress and run the shower. It had been a bad day. Bad. Bad. Bad.

CHAPTER 18

Marc sat in silence in the front room at the Dale. The room was in total darkness, a mood he felt, that matched his soul. Marc knew that the grieving process had begun, what he wondered was how long he would feel this numbness, this empty sense of loss. Although his relationship could be counted in hours rather than weeks or months, he just knew she was the one. Now she was taken from him by a stupid mistake. He should have paid her more attention. Should have made sure that she was close by and he should never have let her wander off like that. All his protocols had been breached. Every single one. He knew that CTO hated civilians or the untrained, as they called them, working in these hostile theatres. However, this was a very important matter. A dirty bomb, a biological weapon, a WMD on a smaller scale.

The Blackberry began to vibrate on the coffee table's glass top. It's screen flashing. Trying to attract Marc's attention. It began to turn slightly as the vibrations stirred it into life. It looked as if it was trying to stand up, arise with a life of it's own. Wearily Marc reached for it.

'Hello'.

'Mr Marc, it's Mr Wilner'.

'Yes sir'.

'Firstly I'm sorry about the blunder to day. The Int guys didn't keep me in the loop. If I thought that they were there I'd have pulled you out'.

The blunder, thought Marc. Was it not something more than a blunder?

'So you had no idea there was a sniper?'

'None at all Marc, none at all'.

'And the gas?'

'Well that's just it. It was water in the flask'.

'Water?', Marc burst out, 'Jenny died for a flask of water?'.

'I'm afraid so'.

'Was there ever any gas?'.

'Oh yes and that's why I'm calling. The second canister, the one we think contains the gas, is now in Scotland. How'd you feel about getting it for us. Think you are up for it?'

'Yes, when?'

'Can you meet the chopper at the playing fields where you normally get it. Don't bring any longs, we're taking care of that?'

'When?'

'Twenty minutes ok?'

'I'll be there'.

'Just one more thing, this is not our operation. It's Military but you have been requested. Specifically asked for. Your partner is the sniper you met earlier to-day'.

There was a silence.

'If you don't wish to take it, that's ok?'

Marc thought for a few seconds then added;

'It's alright Mr Wilner, I will be on the helicopter as soon as'.

The silence returned. The emptiness returned. Marc set the Blackberry down on the coffee table and stood up.

He knew he had to accept this mission, but, he wanted desperately to kill someone and the sniper was number one on his list.

Darkness was falling on Rathcoole. The Abbot knew he would have to leave the flat and seek alternative accommodation. The Saab and the flat were now burned as they say. Rendered useless for him. He knew if military intelligence or CTO or any of the security services were onto him they would find his car and dwelling place sooner or later. He looked at the envelope on the coffee table and reached for it with his good arm. Tipping the contents out, holding the envelope by a corner, it swung in mid air spewing out three passports and several credit and fast cash cards. He had set up these many accounts several years ago when all that was needed was photographic ID and ten pounds. Nowadays, well, now there was a million references and cross checks to be carried out. Still, no one ever looked at the existing accounts.

Gathering up the items he placed them in pairs in his pockets. Each passport had a credit card or a cash card or both, in the corresponding name. Sitting forward on the sofa he gathered up the blue holdall and removed the cardboard box of shotgun cartridges. They were Eagle five hundreds all nine ball shot with a full ounce and a half magnum load. Quite an age yet still viable. The old box was maroon and red with a golden eagle emblazoned on the side. Next he drew out the Franchi SPAS pump action shotgun. It too was old, probably one of the first made. Certainly manufactured before the main combat shotguns came on line. It only held four rounds as it had a shorter barrel than normal. There was no stock, instead a plastic, well worn, pistol grip squatted where stock should be. This particular model had been recalled as the safety catch was unreliable. Nearly all the models were repaired. This one, well, the Abbot had removed it from the dead hands of a Somali warlord he had shot many years ago in Africa. Brought home as a trophy of war, he kept it as a back up for days like this. Days when his back may be against the wall. Days when he would chance the unreliable safety catch. Days when two or three heavy magnum cartridges fired at an enemy might just make the difference. He fed the shells into the greedy magazine. The hollow sound the cylinder made caused him to smile, and smile and smile. Time to go, he thought.

Marc had walked to the playing fields on the Rashee Road in Ballyclare and was opening the gate when he heard the helicopter. It was the same black Bell, with the same pilot and the tall thin figure of the sniper sitting on the left hand side. He stooped and ran underneath the blades. The downdraught rippled down the back of his jacket, it felt like unseen hands trying to rip it off. There was the maelstrom of wind, leaves and debris swirling everywhere and the loud noise of the big engine. That familiar whine accompanied by the constant whup whup of the blades. Climbing inside and closing the door he was greeted by the opposite. Calm, peaceful, plush seats and the green headphones the tall man was reaching him. Placing them over his ears brought almost total silence. Tall man spoke over the head set;

'We are going to Scotland'.

'I know', said Marc dryly.

'How's your friend?'

'Still in surgery I think'.

Tall man turned back to the front. Facing the windscreen, looking out as the pilot spun the now familiar three sixty before flying off. Marc noticed the long black nylon bag propped up on the seat beside him. He wondered if the empty round was still in it's chamber, or had the weapon been stripped and cleaned. His hand moved to the Glock pistol on his belt and he reassuringly touched the pistol grip. I hope this is not going to be a long flight he thought, fixing his gaze on the back of the tall man's head.

The Abbot was standing in his front room, still in the semi darkness, looking around for anything he may have forgotten. He was running a mental check list in his mind, knowing that he would not be returning. The faint scrape of leather on concrete made him freeze. Footstep. They were here. He did not know how he knew this. He just did. His right thumb flicked the safety off on the SPAS. He held his breath. The metallic click of the safety over, he breathed easy. There was a cartridge already in the SPAS, these guns sometimes fired when the safety was activated. This was why he only ever considered this model as a backup.

Straining his ears he could hear nothing else. Now on the balls of his feet he crept to the small kitchen. The frosted glass on the top half of the back door gave little away. Movement. Passing the front window. Caught from the corner of his eye. Shadows. At the rear door too. So a double entry. The distorted torso of a man appeared behind the frosted glass. The handle began to move. Ever so slightly. The door was locked, the key was sticking out underneath the handle, turned sideways. The man was pressing on the door. The glass creaked. Noise was also coming from the front door too. All his senses were straining.

The Abbot grinned. Showtime he muttered under his breath. Then he sprang into action in typical Abbot style. Bringing the SPAS up to waist height he pointed it at the rear door. A smart pull on the trigger, noise, blast, yellow flame. All nine lead balls smashed through the frosted glass as one. Before he had time to see the figure fall the Abbot had racked the SPAS and was running toward the front door. Shots rang out. Two, three, four. Abbot had no idea where they were coming from but he knew he was the intended target.

Reaching the hall he saw the front door smashing inwards. Sliding on his knees he pointed the SPAS and unleashed another shot. He could make out two figures in the doorway. Racking he fired again. There was hesitation then one small man fell forward into the hall. The second dropped his pistol and staggered backward clutching his face. The Abbot sprinted along the hall, hurling himself out into the small garden. He saw a large black car speed off, the wheels spinning as they fought for grip on the tarmac. The rear doors where open and the force of the acceleration closed them loudly. The car rounded the corner within seconds and was lost from sight. Turning now he noticed the second assailant was slumped against the wall of his flat. He was still standing up, but only just. There was blood pouring from his face. He was unarmed. The Abbot walked toward him and back to the house. As he passed the man he pointed the SPAS at his assailant's midriff. The final shot rang out, spinning the man along the wall and onto the grass like a rag doll.

Walking through the house to the rear door the Abbot opened it. A third man lay dead in his rear yard. The Abbot noticed that all three had one common denominator. They were Chinese. He tossed the SPAS back into the coal bunker as he left along the rear path. Cutting through several alleyways he eventually rejoined the main drag near the Diamond. Sirens sounding in the still night air announced the arrival of police or ambulance, or both. There were few people on the street. Everyone looked to their own business here and nothing keeps people indoors like gunshots. Approaching a silver Ford Mondeo taxi the Abbot asked if he was free.

'Aye, where to mate?'

'Holiday Inn, City centre'.

'Jump in mate, no worries'.

Fifteen minutes and twelve pounds later the Abbot was getting out at the Holiday Inn. When the taxi drove off the Abbot walked two streets away to the Dalys Hotel. Here he booked a room and produced one of his many credit cards and passports. A very disinterested receptionist recorded his details and slung a set of heavy keys across the fake mahogany desktop. Her fake smile was matched only by her fake suntan and fake diamond ear rings.

The black Bell helicopter flew low across the Irish Sea and was soon over the Scottish coastline. No one spoke in the dim cabin. Marc could see the green glow of the pilots instruments. After they crossed onto land the pilot called Faslane naval base and requested permission to land. Several minutes later the engine was winding down as Marc and the tall man stepped from the helicopter. The base was windswept and open, much as Marc had remembered it. Scottish cold seeped into his bones and made him shiver. Marc glanced towards the sea bays but could not see the black monsters of the deep that lived there. Long thin black nuclear submarines, with their missiles intact. Slumbering beasts waiting on the masters call to awaken and end this world. Our world. Bringing fire from the sky and that monstrous mushroom cloud signalling total end. Total and forever. The walk was short and soon both stood in the green portacabin that would double as a briefing room. Twin fluorescent tubes cast a stark whiteness on the room, all the windows were covered with black nylon. Very secret thought Marc. There were wooden topped desks and grey plastic chairs aplenty. Marc spun a chair around and sat down. The tall man stood.

CHAPTER 19

The sleepy coastal village of Plocton on the western coast of Scotland sat still and silent in the cool morning air as it had done for hundreds of years. A local postman pulled up in a red van and began his short walk to the houses on Cooper Street. Drawing the bundle of letters out of an old leather satchel, possibly older than the postman himself, he undid the red elastic band holding them together. A black and white border collie dog scurried past him. It's black and white tail sticking out to the side, the gait of the collie was offset so it seemed to be running at an angle. The dog surveyed the postman, their eyes met, but it hurried on past. An old quarrel, long forgotten between the pair, again put to bed. Postie half turned watching the dog as it crossed the road and disappeared from view. He did not know if he felt the dog had made progress or if he felt hurt and deflated that it had not growled at him. Dog's and post men.

His gaze drifted out over the small harbour and he looked at the large white yacht moored a few hundred yards offshore. There were several visitors moorings close to the harbour. Their bright orange lifting buoys and large white and blue marker buoys could be easily seen. A large black 'V' was painted on them to distinguish the visitors moorings from the locals. Each summer hundreds of yachts and large motor boats used these moorings, disgorging crews of all ages and types who row ashore in inflatable dingy or small glass fibre punt to eat and drink in the local public house or hotel or buy provisions from Mrs McTaggart's store. He paid little heed to the three men who were climbing down into a small inflatable which was tied to the white yacht. Turning back to his letters he wondered again about the collie dog, smiling he began his rounds.

Jerome Fielding—Hall opened the door of the portacabin and strolled along the dusty vinyl floor, surveying Marc, the tall man and the helicopter pilot, two of whom were sitting on plastic school chairs. The tall man still stood. Another man small in stature, with a shock of unruly white hair followed Fielding-Hall to the front. He was accompanied by a tall thin blonde girl of little more than twenty five years of age. The pale girl looked as if she was seventeen and due to sit her GCSE exams instead of brief a level two mission. Several rolled up OS maps stuck out from underneath her arm and she carried two heavy looking bags. Marc recognised her as Miss Gail, the white haired man was Mr Wilner. Fielding-Hall spoke;

'Gentlemen. I am Colonel Fielding-Hall for those who do not know me. I'm with Military Intelligence in Whitehall and my two associates are with CTO. As you know the Sarin gas escapade has thrown us a red herring somewhat. It appears that Al Qaeda have been using a group who call themselves Shining Path. Shining Path in turn alerted a Chinese Triad group and CIRA that something biological was coming to Northern Ireland. We were involved in the leak too and so the operation in Ulster to recover the gas was initiated.

However, we have a deep sleeper operative, we call them DESO's, at the minute sitting on what we believe is the Sarin canister. We intend to meet him and swop canisters tonight so that the bomb has no biological capability. Our DESO only relayed us this information a few hours ago. He's been deep cover for several months and communications are rare when at that level of penetration'.

He held out his arm, gesturing Mr Wilner to come forward and then spoke again;

'Mr Wilner from CTO will run through the specifics of the operation'.

Looking directly at the tall man he added,' I wish to speak with you when this is done'.

The tall man nodded.

Mr Wilner and Miss Gail unrolled the OS maps and sea charts on the long classroom table and everyone moved forward for a better view.

'Plocton', began Wilner, 'Is located here. There is a yacht called The Martha moored at the harbour mouth. Inside the yacht are a Shining Path bomb team. We believe the bomb is ninety percent ready to assemble. An old PIRA bomb maker has been on board for three days along with our DESO. Tonight at twenty one hundred hours zulu time the DESO will be rowing ashore to leave the bomb maker on land as his job is done. The DESO will make the return trip alone. As he is doing so Mr Marc you will be rowing ashore. You will hang two white fenders, side by side, on the port side of your punt. This is the signal for the DESO to pass you the canister as his boat passes yours. You in turn will pass the dummy canister to him. If he has been compromised or there is any problem he will place a single blue fender over his port side. That means abort the attempt. Understood?'

Marc nodded.

Mr Wilner ran through the plan one more time before asking Marc for any questions.

'How will I get the punt?'

'You will join a small twenty foot yacht already at sea, which will be mooring in plocton at nineteen hundred or thereabouts. It has one of fielding-Hall's men on board. The punt will be on the visitors mooring as normal.'

'Any codewords for the DESO?'.

'None. The fenders are your only guide. Sound travels far across water and we don't wish to alert anyone'.

'What make is the Martha, length, specification . . . .' Marc's voice trailed off as Mr Wilner reached him an A four sheet with all the yachts specifications listed and an accompanying photograph attached.

Briefly scanning the document he found the yacht was a forty foot Jeanneau with a fifty three foot mast and enough room to sleep eight on board. Marc was a gifted sailor and was well acquainted with this type of yacht. Looking at Mr Wilner Marc asked;

'And what of the small boat I'm joining?'

Wilner smiled,' It's a simple little nineteen foot Caprice day sailer'.

'Crew?'

'Only one on board. You will make two. Nice and cosy eh?'

Marc nodded, imagining the small, cramped sailing boat and an unknown associate.

'The sniper will cover you from the high headland to the north of the harbour, just in case it goes Pete Tong so to speak', continued Mr Wilner.

Marc smiled, 'In case of a Cluster?'

'In case of a cluster. Marc we really need this to work. The PM and the cabinet are on the spit if this gas escapes or we get a contaminated blast somewhere'.

Marc nodded.

Everyone was going over their particular tasks and engrossed studying maps, charts and relevant data. No one noticed the tall man slipping outside along with Fielding-Hall.

On the wooden steps that led to the portacabin's front door Fielding-Hall grabbed the tall man's arm and whispered;

'Listen, no one outside ourselves knows the identity of the DESO. If the CTO man speaks with him or you get a chance drop him, we clear?'

'Is he not on our side?'

'Let me worry about the fallout. There is too much riding on this to allow anyone to fuck it up'.

The tall man nodded.

'So you are clear, drop the CTO operative when the job is done'.

The tall man nodded again.

A few hours later Marc and the tall man watched the helicopter fly off after it's three sixty. Walking down the roughly hewn wooden steps at the quayside they boarded a Royal Navy rib, which was rising and falling rapidly as the tide washed it every few seconds. There was a plastic cover over the rib, partly to conceal it's cargo and partly to protect the crew from the elements. Seconds after they boarded the rib's one hundred and ten horsepower Honda outboard spluttered into life. The bow rose and the stern dropped and the rib headed seaward. Marc looked at the white water wake the big engine kicked up as he settled back in his seat. Tall man sat across from him. Still there had been little conversation.

Marc watched the small Caprice grow bigger and bigger as the rib approached it at thirty five knots. He had never sailed a Caprice but he had, for many years sailed a selection of twenty and twenty five foot dayboats. He liked their small compact cabins and the fact that everything was within reach and tightly packet together. Cutting the engine at the last minute allowed the rib to kiss the starboard side of the small yacht. Marc stood up, throwing his bag to a pale looking man in the small boats cockpit then grabbing the shroud he stepped on board. The pale sailor muttered something about charts and tea and stepped off onto the rib. Some confusion arose and there was a debate between the tall man and the now paler sailor. The tall man pulled the plastic door to the side and shouted to Marc;

'He's sea sick. You OK on your own?'

Marc nodded. Seconds later the rib was gone. Marc knew it would drop the tall man on the western side of the headland and he would make his way to a position where he could cover the handover. It would then drop the sea sick sailor back at the quay where Marc and the tall man had boarded. This same rib was going to take Marc's real flask, containing the gas, to a Royal Navy ship where a science officer would check the components.

Opening his bag Marc checked again that he had the flask Fielding-Hall had given him. There were other items there too, his Glock nine millimetre pistol, spare mags, mobile phone in a watertight container and a heavy sailing jacket. Rummaging in the bag he found a bearing compass and a hand held GPS. Marc found the charts below in the saloon and brought them up to the cockpit. Three bearings taken, he worked out where he was on the chart then confirmed it with his GPS. A small five horsepower Tohatsu outboard was ticking over on the transom at the aft of the craft. Marc judged the distance he had to go and the wind speed and decided to sail the Caprice around the headland and onto it's mooring. With that he unfurled the foresail, set the main and cut the engine. Within minutes the small, graceful craft was showing a steady five knots on the log as she sliced through the wash. Marc smiled for the first time in a while. Perhaps the sail would lift his mind.

The tall man made his way up through the heather and gorse bushes, sometimes using the path, sometimes tramping the grasses as he looked for a good vantage point. It was his choice, where he observed from, where he would shoot from, how he would enter and exit the spot. Years of experience were carried with ease by the tall man. In all this time he never had any feelings for the targets. He knew that they all had done something bad to bring him to their door. Targeting was his speciality, easy in, easy out and a body or two in the middle. However, the last job, the quarry job, lay heavy on his mind. He admired Marc but he felt his anger and was weary of him. He could feel the hatred there sometimes, not like the twenty four seven mixture of hatred and indifference he felt in Ulster when he worked there. But a hatred strong enough, none the less. At last he reached a point where he could see the harbour and with very little movement he could also see the open sea beyond the headland. Looking through his monocular he spotted the Caprice only a few miles away and sailing steadily towards the moorings. He watched Marc as he steered with the tiller and set the mainsail every now and then. He is a remarkable man he thought. Truly remarkable.

A few short hours later Marc was approaching the visitors buoy as briefed. There was a small fibreglass punt tied to the mooring. Visitors used these punts to get ashore as not all yachts carried tenders. Every few days the old harbour master would check on them and at the end of the season they were brought ashore for winter storage. The caprice was still under sail, quietly and stealthily the little boat approached the mooring. Marc furled the foresail and the boats speed dropped to little more than a knot. With a firm grip on the aluminium, telescopic boathook, Marc leaned out and caught the lifting buoy. At the same time he released the main sheet allowing the mainsail to spill wind. The Caprice stopped and began to turn head to wind. Marc pulled the lifting buoy and the attached rope into the cockpit, wrapping it around the cleat he made fast and secured the small craft.

Checking his watch Marc saw it was eight thirty, he had half an hour to kill before there would be any movement from the Martha. He slipped below deck into the tiny cramped saloon and looked through his night binoculars. There, bathed in a green light, he saw the Martha. Sweeping along her deck and cockpit he could see no one but there were lights burning in the aft cabin and the saloon. Marc watched for several minutes but nothing changed. Eventually he re-emerged into the cockpit and opened the aft locker. Here he found several white plastic fenders with ropes attached. Designed to be hung along the side of the small craft they would stop it rubbing on any jetty or pontoon or even another boat and causing damage. He drew out two fairly new looking, white, plastic fenders and tossed them into the punt which he had pulled close to the Caprice and tied off. Movement caught his eye and he glanced toward the larger yacht a few hundred yards away. He saw two men getting into a small glass fibre punt, casting off and rowing towards the shore.

The tall man saw them too. He placed his earpiece in his left ear, the dialled a mobile number. It was answered by silky voice, Fielding-Hall himself;

'Yes?'

'Two men in small boat heading shore bound'.

'Is the CTO boat there?'

'Yes that's a roger'.

'Can you see DESO?'

'Yes that's a roger'.

'Just keep eyes on. Keep me in the loop'.

When the small punt reached the shore it bumped into the old row of tyres along the harbour wall. Rising and falling gently with the tidal lap of the sea. Marc watched as a man climbed out. He straightened up and walked briskly to a parked car. Watching still he saw him fumble in his pocket, then enter the car. Several seconds later it started up, lights on, and off it drove. Marc watched the two red orbs getting smaller and smaller until they disappeared.

CHAPTER 20

Marc swung his legs into the small punt and gathered up the oars and oar locks. A swift hand nimbly untied the painter and he pushed the punt away from the Caprice. Rocking gently back and forth he pulled the oars through the brine with ease. The punt stabilized and gathered speed, heading shoreward. After a few minutes Marc stopped and glanced over his shoulder to check his direction and get a rough position for the out bound boat. He had tied the fenders side by side to the port cleat and he gently tipped them over the port side. His observation showed him no fenders of any kind on the out bound boat.

Tall man spoke softly on the mobile;

'Boats are almost alongside'.

'Good good'.

'Transfer completed'.

'Confirm CTO has got the goods?'

'I can confirm, I say again I can confirm'.

'Outstanding. Ok you are to keep eyes on until I contact you again'.

'What about the other task. When do want me to take target?'.

'Negative, I have the matter in hand'.

'Confirm you no longer wish target terminated'.

'That is correct. I have the matter in hand'.

Tall man's phone went dead. He puzzled over the call, although he had reservations regarding the hit he knew that Fielding-Hall would not. He was not happy about this latest twist, not by a long way.

Marc waited until the small boat was beside his. The man rowing it paused, half turned, then a black flask dropped into Marc's punt. At the same time Marc reached over and deposited his flask on the floor of the small boat. The rower avoided eye contact and pulled away gently and steadily. Marc turned his small rowing boat hard to starboard and rowed in a giant circle back to the Caprice. Setting the flask into the boat he clambered in too. With the punt tied to the mooring rope, Marc dropped the five horsepower outboard into the water. It was primed and ready to start. He hoisted the mainsail and slipped the mooring rope off. Quietly and steadily the small sailing boat left it's moorings and headed out to sea. After he was quite a distance from the moorings Marc fired up the outboard, dropped the mainsail and motored toward the headland.

Tall man was still on the headland watching Marc depart. He was scanning the sea to the west when he saw the white wake of a powerful motorboat approaching. He guessed it would be fifteen or twenty minutes before both boats met. He scrolled down his phone menu and dialled a number.

Marc's Blackberry was ringing, digging underneath his lifejacket he released it from the inside pocket of his fleece lined sailing jacket.
'Hello'.

'Mr Marc?'

'Yes'

'Something is wrong. I think you should check your boat'.

Marc recognised the voice as that of the tall mans.

'For what?'

'I had a second task tonight, that task was you. I was to take you out, but now it's been binned'.

'Oh. So why are you telling me this?'

'I know you hate me for shooting the girl. I have no beef with you but I don't want you following me for ever and trying to even the score.'

Marc's blood ran cold.

'You still there?' asked tall man.

'Yes'.

'You have three men in a rib, about two miles to your west. Look like marines or Royal Navy. Reckon they are your RV'.

'Thanks', stuttered Marc.

'goodbye'.

The Blackberry rang off and then rang again almost immediately.

'Hello'.

'Hi, Marc?'

'Yes, go ahead'.

'Fielding-Hall here. All Ok. You get the item?'

'Oh yes. Item all secure'.

'Grand. Grand. An RN rib is waiting for you at open sea. Transfer the item then return to the harbour moorings. Bit of a change of plan'.

'Oh. How so?'.

'Just ring me when your tied up. I will explain then?'

Again the phone rang off.

Marc looped a rope around the wooden tiller and tied the Caprice onto a straight path. Bolting into the cockpit he began a frantic search. Lifting the cushions he checked the two compartments on the port side. Flares, anchor and chain, first aid box and bolt cutters, nothing out of place. Turning to the other side he lifted the cushions and then the wooden hatch covers. There sitting among the pots and pans was a Tupperware box. It had a small rubber aerial sticking out from it's lid, which was sealed with tape. A cheap mobile phone was taped to the other side of the box. He did not need to look inside it. Marc had seen undercar booby trap bombs before and this was of a very similar construction. Marc guessed the explosive was commercial. Semtex or C4 maybe. He dropped the lid on the hatch and replaced the cushions. He knew if he tried to remove the bomb or open the box with a view to defusing it, that it would explode. Somewhere there would be an anti handling device attached, Marc visualised a thin sliver of nylon cat gut on the underside of the Tupperware container. He imagined lifting the box and the cat gut tugging the wooden dowel out from the jaws of a wooden clothes peg allowing the drawing pin contacts to connect. He shivered at the thought again.

Replacing the wooden hatch he returned to the cockpit. The Caprice was holding her own at a steady five knots. From the fuse board on the port side of the cabin he flicked on the navigation lights. Quite a distance away the Royal Marines spotted the red and green glow. They had been watching for any signal and now they had it. The rib altered course and made for the headland and away from any prying eyes at the harbour.

Marc cut the outboard as the rib approached. It had been close to an hour since he had found the device and he had been sweating although the night was cold. The camouflaged face of a Royal Marine appeared at the side of the Caprice.

'Alright mate, are you Marc?' asked the tall slim marine.

'Yep that's me'

'You got a package then?'

Marc had placed the flask in his bag, he held it up and the Marine grabbed it. Then Marc sprang onto the rib landing beside the marine.

'No no mate. You stay with the sail boat'. Said the startled marine.

'Change of plan'. Marc insisted, 'I got to accompany the package'. The two marines had a Chinese parliament at the far side of the rib then approached Marc.

'Ok then mate', said the shorter, fatter one. 'Better grab a seat'.

With that the rib sped off leaving the Caprice in its wake bobbing about like a cork in a bath.

Tall mans mobile rang a short time later;

'You still got eyes on?' asked silky voice.

'Yes I do'.

'Has the package been given to the Navy?'

'That's correct'.

'CTO still on sailing boat'.

'That's affirmative'. Lied tall man.

'Do you like fireworks?'

Tall man did not answer. Far away from the harbour and the headland silky voice was dialling another number on another mobile. It Rang.

Seconds later the Caprice exploded into tiny fragments. There was a brief fireball, black smoke and debris scattered over several hundred yards. The engine and mast sank almost immediately. Large chunks of fibreglass floated for a few minutes before sinking beneath the waves. Floating debris soon became dispersed and began to follow the tide. Soon nothing would remain to prove the existence of the Caprice at all.

'Did I hear a bang?' asked silky voice, 'Sounded like a gas explosion on a yacht?'

'Yachts destroyed', replied tall man.

'Good. Mission over, return to base'.

The tall man gathered his equipment and walked off in the direction of Plocton. There should be a car hidden in the town somewhere for his use. He felt better having warned Marc of the set up. Although he had no direct knowledge he had a fair idea that Fielding-Hall would make sure anyone who had contact with the DESO would not live to tell the tale. No loose ends. Ever. The tall man knew that when they were finished with his services for good at some point a similar fate awaited him. He was glad therefore that he had a one way ticket to Australia back in his flat. This just might be the time to visit his brother in Queensland.

An RFA ship, the Largs Bay, loomed out of the water in front of the rib. Travelling for thirty minutes across the sea the rib was fast approaching it's home base. She was a bay class, manned by the Royal Fleet Auxiliary. The Royal Navy's version of the Merchant Navy thought Marc. It had been many years since he had been on board a bay class. The rib cut engine close to the ship and bumped alongside. It towered out of the water making the rib seem even smaller. Like a great grey block of flats, a tall tower block, cold and wet, floating on the sea. For a second Marc wondered how something this big could possibly float. A wooden ladder was lowered from the Pilot hatch on the ships side. Marc could make out the yellow glow of light marking the hatch opening. He followed the tall marine up the ladder and was helped into the bowels of the ship by a pair of eager, waiting hands.

An older man wearing white overalls stepped forward. He introduced himself as Mike and enquired after the package. Marc delved into his bag and handed the flask to him. There were no insignia or name badges on his coveralls, Marc knew immediately he was a Porton down man.

A short time later Marc stood in the main communications office, or radio shack as it was better known. The scientist, still in his white coveralls handed a signals communication to the radio officer on duty. He scanned the signals form two two six, making sure the ship's captain had signed it then passed it to the communications rating for transmission. The female, blonde rating quickly typed the message which simply read;

'Mother is home, can confirm a baby boy, safe and well'.

At CTO headquarters Mr Christian stared at the message, then lifting the handset began to ring all the numbers listed on his screen. It took forty minutes to inform all the recipients. All the important people from the Prime Minister to Mr Wilner. The Sarin threat was, for now, not imminent.

On board the Largs Bay Marc climbed into the rear of the Lynx helicopter. Pilot and navigator ran through their series of checks and soon were airborne. Marc had spoken to Wilner on the secure Brent phone earlier and informed him of the double cross and the bomb. He deliberately left out the tall man's part in the whole scenario, simply saying that he had located the device. Wilner had told him that he was not at all surprised, having worked with FRU and Fielding-Hall before. Marc was instructed to return to the Dale and stay off the radar for a few days while Wilner and the powers that be tried to sort something out. As the helicopter flew across the Irish sea the navigator reached a laptop to Marc.

'Thought you might like to have some in-flight entertainment', he added.

Marc smiled. The navigator reached a set of small, i-pod sized, headphones to Marc.

'Just press play', he shouted.

Marc attached the head phones and clicked the mouse onto play. A video began on the laptop's screen. It was of helicopters flying in Iraq, Afghanistan and the USA. They were video clips made from cameras and mobile telephones. Obviously taken by servicemen in the on going conflicts. Music began to play through the headset. It was Walking in the Air, from The Snowman. The angelic music was in stark contrast to the images onscreen. There were wounded servicemen being loaded, flown and unloaded from various helicopters. Some choppers were attacking enemy positions, the GPMG machine guns were firing tracer rounds and there was a final clip of several rockets being fired by an Apache attack helicopter.

Flicking the laptop off, Marc stared out over the inky blackness of the sea. His thoughts returned to Jenny and the dreadful unfolding of the quarry incident began to play in his mind, much like the laptop video. Try as he might he could not get the Snowman out of his head. It played over and over, he found himself fighting the urge to sing along. Looking down at his wrist he stared at the bracelet, hard to make out in the dull glow inside the Lynx. His left hand felt for it. Squeezed it reassuringly. Feeling its solid metal grip. Knowing it would never let go, just like he would never let go of Jenny's memory. This had to be a bad dream.

Slipping the large headphones on Marc asked if they could land him at Antrim Area Hospital instead of RAF Aldergrove. Both agreed that this would be no trouble. Twenty five minutes later Marc was making his way to the ICU ward to check on Jay.

In his hotel room in the Holiday Inn at Stoke on Trent, the Abbot answered his new Nokia cell phone. The message he received was short, detailed and very to the point. The caller rang off without giving the Abbot time to reply. Looking at his one remaining Mauser nine millimetre on the dresser, the Abbot smiled. Life was a funny old thing he thought. Who would have thought he would get such a gift at this time. Soon, he thought, the matter will be settled.

Marc stayed with Jay a long time. He dozed in the comfy chair in the relatives room for a short while when Jay's dressings were changed. Returning to sit with him when nurses allowed. They talked little. Jay asked after Jenny and was saddened by the news. Both men talked of FRU and the boat bomb and what they should do. As Marc went to leave Jay reached out his hand. Marc held it. Then turning towards him Jay whispered;

'I'm truly sorry about Jenny Marc. I know she was special'.

Marc nodded.

'And you say Fielding-Hall had her shot by that sniper guy?'

Marc nodded again.

'In my jacket pocket', he said pointing, 'A mobile phone'.

'Your Blackberry is in the Dale'.

'No this is an old Nokia'.

Marc rummaged in the jacket pocket and produced an ancient Nokia. He pushed it into Jay's hand.

'Now; said Jay,' Get home and get some sleep'.

Marc bid his farewell and walked off down the corridor. Jay fired up the old phone and scrolled the menu, finding a long disused number. He knew Fielding-Hall and his teams would never give up. Eventually they would locate Marc and complete the task in hand.

CHAPTER 21

AFTERMATH

Marc scanned through the old newspapers in the airport departure lounge. Week old headlines telling of a three man bomb team caught in Manchester close to the Trafford shopping centre. A specialist police unit arresting the men after a short shoot out. The article told of a bomb in a back pack, but made no mention of a canister of Sarin gas or indeed anything more than a plain old bomb. Full details on pages three to five it promised. Marc had seen the breaking news story on CNN and the BBC back at the Dale the morning after he visited Jay. Two more arrests had been made in Scotland when a yacht was boarded and a man had been picked up at Stranraer as he drove a car onto the ferry. All were linked to Shining Path in one way or another. Marc knew all but the DESO would go to prison.

Jay sat across from him in the deeper, more comfortable chairs. He was still far from fully recovered but had been allowed this flight and journey to Jenny's funeral.

Outside the small country church Mr Wilner greeted Jay and Marc with a firm handshake. Looking at Marc he started;

'Fielding-Hall's here. I've spoken to everyone, even the PM in chambers but he's well protected. So I simply told him that you were picked up after the yacht sank when the gas tank exploded. We will have to be on our toes for a while. He is a dangerous man'.

With that Fielding-Hall approached the group on foot.

'Wilner good to see you'.

'Mr Fielding-Hall', said all three men together. There were the customary false handshakes. As he shook Marc's hand he paused;

'So, your boat had a gas explosion eh?'

'Indeed it did sir'.

'Well you are a lucky young man. Grand result, you did a good job, all the same. Nation owes you all a great debt. Well done what'.

Turning on his heel he made his way into the church shaking hands and greeting people as he went. Marc remembered little of the service. There were flowers and some weeping girl friends at the front of the church. A young vicar delivered a watery service about flowers growing up and being cut down and his fathers house having many mansions. It all washed over Marc as the sea washes over rocks on the beach. He found himself thinking back to their lovemaking. Her laughter. Chasing her around the Dale. Her eyes. He reached with his left hand feeling the bracelet on his right. Rubbing it comforted him somehow.

Soon the service was over. The church began to empty it's congregation walking to the door in a steady, small, thin line. Fielding-Hall marched out of the church grounds and toward the black Mercedes car with it's waiting driver. Glancing in Marc's direction and pondering the best way to tie up his loose ends. He clambered into the rear seat as the driver held open the door. No acknowledgement was made. It was expected. A man in his position, a powerful man did not speak with a mere driver.

'Back home', he barked.

'Very good sir', said the driver, with a flat but well disguised Belfast accent.

Jay paused at the church door and observed the Mercedes and the driver. He smiled but remained silent, then helped by Marc he limped away to the waiting taxi.

Fielding-Hall's car was found two days later in an alleyway behind a public house in Kendal. Two young boys playing had located it. His upright body had two nine millimetre holes to the forehead. The last sound he ever heard was the Abbot saying ;

'Boute ye big man?', as he half turned in the drivers seat before letting his silenced Mauser do it's job.

Marc often wondered about the hit.

Wilner often wondered too, but knew now that it was truly over.

Jay often wondered how his old contact had still been able to reach the Abbot, after all these years.

The Abbot? Well he never wondered at all. Not ever.

GLOSSARY

Bout Ye; Belfast slang for 'What about you' or' How are you'. Often used as a greeting.

CIRA; Republican breakaway group with some ex PIRA members.

Coole; Belfast slang for Rathcoole, a large housing estate on the outskirts of Belfast.

C.T.O. Counter terrorist operations or counter terrorist operatives. May also be referred to as 'The Firm', Used by MI5/MI6 as black operations.

FRU; Force Research Unit, a British Army undercover unit used in Northern Ireland in the seventies. Not much is known about their methods or results.

Gnat. Cannabis type narcotic grown and smoked mainly in Africa.

INLA; Irish National Liberation Army. Republican terrorist group.

Longs; Slang for long weapons, rifles etc.

MOD; Ministry of Defence.

MP; Military Police.

NATO Standard; Slang term for tea with milk and two sugars.

Nines; Slang term for nine millimetre rounds.

Nutted; Belfast slang term for 'shot in the head', also known as a 'head job'.

OP: Military term for observation post, normally concealed.

Pete Tong; Slang for something having gone wrong.

Provos; Slang term for Provisional IRA, (PIRA) also known in Belfast as 'The Ra'.

PSNI; Police Service of Northern Ireland.

SA80; Current British Army standard issue rifle.

SAS; Special Air Service. British Army special forces, may also be referred to as 'The Regiment', 'Troop' or 'Det'.

Squaddie; Slang term for soldier.

TSG; Technical Support Group, PSNI's public order police.

UVF; Ulster Volunteer Force, loyalist terrorist group.

CPSIA information can be obtained at www.ICGtesting.com
Printed in the USA
BVOW041002201011

274143BV00001B/41/P

9 781456 793739